"I need a woman."

"Really?" Abby said with a snap.

"You've seen the apartment." Emilio spread his hands. "I need someone to furnish it."

"So employ an interior decorator."

"I did. That was him on the phone this evening. I fired him."

"I heard. Maybe you ought to call him back and unfire him."

He looked at her pleadingly. "You can stay as long as you like. You solve my problem, I solve yours." He held out his hand across the table.

Abby took it reluctantly. She had a nasty feeling that a whole portfolio of new problems was about to open up in front of her....

Born in London, **Sophie Weston** is a traveler by nature who started writing when she was five. She wrote her first romance recovering from illness, thinking her traveling was over. She was wrong, but she enjoyed it so much that she has carried on. These days she lives in the heart of the city with two demanding cats and a cherry tree—and travels the world looking for settings for her stories.

Look out for
The Millionaire's Daughter and *The Bridesmaid's Secret*
by Sophie Weston

Don't miss these thrilling stories
about two very different sisters and the men they marry—
on sale in January and February 2002!

Books by Sophie Weston

MORE THAN A MILLIONAIRE

Sophie Weston

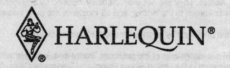

HARLEQUIN®

TORONTO • NEW YORK • LONDON
AMSTERDAM • PARIS • SYDNEY • HAMBURG
STOCKHOLM • ATHENS • TOKYO • MILAN • MADRID
PRAGUE • WARSAW • BUDAPEST • AUCKLAND

ISBN 0-373-03677-9

MORE THAN A MILLIONAIRE

First North American Publication 2001.

Copyright © 2001 by Sophie Weston.

This edition published by arrangement with Harlequin Books S.A.

® and TM are trademarks of the publisher. Trademarks indicated with
® are registered in the United States Patent and Trademark Office, the
Canadian Trade Marks Office and in other countries.

Visit us at www.eHarlequin.com

Printed in U.S.A.

CHAPTER ONE

IT WAS a perfect Saturday afternoon at the Hacienda Montijo. Glamorous guests had enjoyed a long lazy lunch. Now they strolled through the famous gardens or drowsed over English tea on the lawn. Children romped in the swimming pool. The sun shone. Bees hummed.

The shy English visitor refused to be shifted from the terrace out into the sunshine, though.

'Wouldn't you like to go and mingle, Abby?' said her hostess, without much hope.

'No, I'll just stay here and watch. If that's all right,' said the English girl politely.

Her hostess sighed and gave up. She was watching, too.

For below them, on the velvet-smooth tennis court, a battle to the death was in progress. A tall blond giant was sweating profusely as his opponent slammed him all around the court.

The dark tennis player was like quicksilver. He moved all the time, fast as a jaguar, graceful as a dancer. It seemed that wherever his opponent sent the ball, he was there first, totally in control.

'Who is that?' said the Montijo matriarch in displeasure. The blond giant was her favourite grandson.

She shifted in her cane chair and her daughter-in-law sighed inwardly. She signalled to her husband across the lawn. Why wasn't he here when she needed him? He *knew* this was going to be difficult. He had no business leaving her to deal with it. Especially not as she was struggling to entertain the monosyllabic English girl at the same time.

She said brightly, 'That's Emilio Diz, Mama.'

The matriarch stiffened. 'Diz?'

The English girl turned her head. She was a teenager; she

should have been with the other teenagers, thought Annaluisa Montijo despairingly. But she was too tall and gangly to interest the boys and too suffocatingly shy to talk to the girls. So she ended up here in the middle of what was about to become a nasty family row.

'Which one is Emilio Diz?' she asked politely.

Both older women stared at her. Blond Bruno Montijo was the son and heir. The house was full of photographs of him, posed and unposed, muddy and magnificent on a polo pony, sleek and glamorous in black evening clothes at balls and receptions and premieres. His cups for fencing filled a cabinet in the library. He was rich, he was gorgeous and, inevitably, he was a national celebrity. Even if she did not recognise the world-class tennis player, the English girl should have recognised blond and gorgeous Bruno on his own home territory. It was almost an insult to the family not to. The matriarch drew an outraged breath.

Her daughter-in-law rushed into speech. 'Of course, you haven't met Bruno yet, Abby.' She sent her mother-in-law a pleading look. 'He's my oldest son. The fair one.'

'And the other really is Emilio Diz?' said Abby, unaware of digging herself into a deeper hole.

The matriarch glared.

Her daughter-in-law intervened quickly. 'Are you a fan, Abby?' She tried hard to sound amused.

Where was Felipe? She caught sight of her husband and sent him another, more urgent, signal.

'Of course she isn't a fan,' snapped the matriarch. 'She didn't know what the wretched man even looked like.'

'No,' admitted Abby, blushing.

Caught out again, she thought. This last week had been a nightmare. She seemed to have lurched from one social mistake to the next. She had never imagined people could make so many rules just to live day to day—or that she could find so many ways to break them.

She tried to explain that she wasn't showing off about

something she didn't really understand. 'I've heard my brothers talk about him. They thought he would be Wimbledon champion this year if he hadn't retired from the circuit.'

But even that was wrong.

'The circuit,' sniffed the matriarch. 'In my day lawn tennis was played by gentlemen. Not circus animals.'

Her daughter-in-law winced. Abby blushed harder and hung her head.

'Oh, be fair, Mama,' said the daughter-in-law, with compassion for this ugly duckling who always seemed to say the wrong thing, 'Emilio Diz is a great tennis player and a national hero.'

'Humph. Then why isn't he still playing tennis? He's only, what is it? Twenty-five? Twenty-six? Plenty of time to win something worthwhile. Why has he given up and gone into business?' She spat the last words out as if they were obscene.

'They say he's very intelligent...' protested the daughter-in-law faintly.

'That's why Felipe sold him the Palacio Azul, is it?' said the matriarch with rancour.

The daughter-in-law knew when she was out of her depth. She looked round for help. It came puffing up the terrace steps.

'For a very fair price, Mama,' said Felipe Montijo, arriving slightly out of breath. 'Unlike us, he has the resources to develop the place into a full sports complex...'

The matriarch swung her dark glasses round on him for an unnerving moment. 'Develop? The house your grandfather built?'

'It's falling down, Mama. We can't afford...'

'And this man can?'

'Oh, he can, all right,' said Felipe with feeling. 'He wasn't just a tennis player, even when he was a professional. He made a killing on entertainment event software. Now he's going into property in a big way.'

'New money!' Rosa Montijo was shocked and did not attempt to disguise it. 'And you ask him to your home? Let him meet Rosanna?'

Felipe laughed. 'He's not interested in Rosanna, Mama. He's twenty-five and he's been on the international tennis circuit since he was eighteen, for heaven's sake. He dates movie stars, not high school girls.'

'In my day we would never have introduced the daughter of the house to a man like that.'

Her daughter-in-law intervened. 'Felipe is doing business with him, Mama. Of course we ask him.'

The matriarch was disdainful. 'His mother used to work for my hairdresser.'

Montijo husband and wife exchanged despairing looks.

Watching silently, Abby saw it with interest. It was the first time this pleasant husband and wife had shown any signs of communicating. They had been very hospitable but there was a coldness at the heart of this house. It worried her. She did not know how to deal with it. Probably that was what made her even more clumsy and tactless than all those rules she kept falling over.

Abby looked across the perfect lawn to the distant tennis court. A cluster of beautifully dressed people were grouped outside the netting, watching the match with palpable excitement. But it was not the fashionable crowd that brought Abby's heavy brows together in a worried frown. It was not even the duel on court. It was that coldness.

Maybe that is what Daddy meant, when he said they were sophisticated, thought Abby. She sighed.

She knew she was not sophisticated. If she hadn't already known it, the friends of her host's daughter would have made her realise it. Their sexy clothes made her blink. And their knowing conversation silenced her. It was like watching one of the international soap operas that they all loved.

Abby never managed to see the glamorous soap operas, though most of them were aired in England. They were for-

bidden at her boarding school. And at home she was too
busy, mucking out the stables, tearing into the overgrown
garden or doing what she could to patch up the worst decayed
bits of the Palladian pile that was her home.

Her father would hug her and say she was a good girl but
she knew that he was worried about her. Abby did not see
why. She was perfectly happy. Well, maybe not perfectly.
But as long as the west wing roof did not leak this winter,
she had not got much to wish for, she thought.

Her noisy siblings treated her as if she was a fifth brother.
The village generally behaved as if she was an apprentice
workman, teaching her various tricks of carpentry and plumb-
ing whenever the latest disaster struck the Hall. As for the
county, now that she was sixteen, they either asked her to
dinner as her widowed father's partner for the evening or
froze her out, as an impediment to his—in their view—long
overdue remarriage.

It was the dinner parties that Abby hated. That was why
her father had brought her on this business trip with him to
Argentina.

She protested. Of course she protested. There was too
much to do before Christmas. The pipes might freeze if she
was not there to make sure that proper steps were taken when
the temperature dropped. She would only be in the way.

'But I really want you to meet the Montijos.'

Then they could come to Yorkshire in the summer when
there was no possibility of freeze or flood.

'Yes, and they will. But first I'd like you to stay with them.
Señora Montijo is a very sophisticated woman. As well as
very kind. See what you can learn from her, Smudge.'

'Learn from her?' said Abby, wary but disarmed by the
nursery nickname.

'Clothes and things,' said her father vaguely.

There was nothing wrong with Abby's clothes that a
healthy increase in her allowance wouldn't put right. But she
was too fond of her father to say so. Four sons of super

intelligence and expensive hobbies had depleted his resources almost as much as the roof. He worked hard and travelled the world. He made a good income. But the house and the family between them kept pace. There was never much left over for Abby.

Fortunately, so far she had been happy to live in jeans, topped off by shirts and sweaters that she found in the boys' catalogues of sports and adventure wear. This was the first time she had realised that her father was not as happy with this wardrobe as she was.

'You want me to be more feminine,' she said, depressed. 'Curls and stuff.'

Her father smiled affectionately and ruffled her soft dark hair, currently caught of her eyes in a raggedy pony-tail. 'Please God, no.'

'Well, then—'

'You need a woman to show you how to deal with people, darling.'

'Oh, come, Pops. We've done sex at school,' said Abby dryly. 'If we hadn't, it would be a bit late now, don't you think?'

He looked uncomfortable. 'Not just sex.'

'All right, what then?'

'I suppose—social know-how.'

'Social know-how?' Abby was incredulous. She primmed up her mouth and minced across the room in a very fair imitation of a catwalk model. 'How to get out of a sports car without showing too much leg? Come into the real world, Pops. Anyway, you don't think there's any such thing as too much leg,' she added practically.

Abby thought he would laugh. He didn't. He smiled, but absently. It was obvious that he was really worried.

'Oh, Smudge. If only it was as simple as that.'

Abby began to feel alarmed. 'I don't understand.'

'I know you don't. That's part of the problem.' He sighed.

'You're such an open person, Smudge. You're honest and it never occurs to you that other people may not be.'

She shook her head, even more bewildered.

'I'm no good at this,' he said, angry with himself. 'If your mother were alive she would explain. It's about learning how to talk to people. How to listen. How to hear what they really mean. Not just what they say. That sort of social know-how.'

'You make it sound like learning another language,' she scoffed.

But inside she was alarmed. She had not seen her father so serious since Will had disappeared in the Himalayas for three weeks before he was found safe and well in totally the wrong valley. Surely her social inadequacies were not in the same class? She very nearly said so.

But her father was struggling to put his worries into words. 'It is a bit. And like a language, you just have to practice. Only you don't. You're a sweetheart and you look after the boys and me like someone twice your age. But—you haven't the slightest idea how to walk into a room and mingle.' He gave a sharp sigh. 'You're so shy. I don't know what to do about it. Annaluisa Montijo is the best solution I can think of.'

'Oh.'

'Your mother always said there were going to be too many men in your life. I'm beginning to realise what she meant,' he said ruefully.

He smiled in that way he always did when he talked about his dead wife to his daughter. It was as if she was standing just behind Abby's shoulder and he was laughing into her eyes. The intimacy was breathtaking. So was the sense of loss.

When he looked like that, Abby would do anything for him. Even go to a country where she knew no one, did not speak the language and had no idea what she would do all day while her father was at his meetings. Abby was not good with strangers.

And, though she did her best to disguise it whenever her father came out to the hacienda, this lot were way out of her ken. She *had* been more miserable—her first week at school, for example—but she had never felt so utterly surplus to requirements. She knew that her hostess wanted her to make friends with her daughter. But Rosanna Montijo and her smart friends, although they were only a year older than Abby, felt like another generation. She went to their dances and barbecues and counted the hours until she could persuade one of the chauffeurs to give her a lift home. She never managed to mingle.

The only place she felt really happy at Hacienda Montijo was the stables. That was odd because, of all her family, she was the one who was secretly nervous of horses. But here the gauchos had patience with her slow Spanish and the horses, perverse creatures as always, were pleased to see her.

This Saturday's lunch party was an ordeal. She bore it by reminding herself that she was returning home for Christmas in three days' time. All she had to do was avoid Rosanna and Rosanna's friends today and she would be on the homeward stretch.

Accordingly, she pleaded aversion to the powerful sun and stayed firmly on the terrace. This threw her in to company with the older Montijos. It was not easy, with the women speaking courteous English for her benefit and clearly wishing she was anywhere else.

But it couldn't be helped. In three days' time she would be gone and could forget the whole beastly business: sophisticated seventeen-year-olds; international tennis stars that weren't good enough for the Montijos; chilly family dinners; the lot. And she could go back to being grubby Abby Templeton Burke. After all, you didn't need to be sophisticated to do basic repairs to the ancestral home.

'Do you not play tennis, Abby?' asked her hostess with a touch of desperation.

'No.'

'But you said your brothers like it?'

'They're good at it,' said Abby with simple truth.

'Oh. And you're not?' asked kind Felipe. 'Well, it doesn't really matter. I'm sure you're good at lots of other things.'

'Not games. My brother Will says I can't catch a ball to save my life.'

The matriarch did not like being ignored.

'That man is showing off,' she announced, pointing her gold-topped stick at the tennis court.

'It's not showing off if you're world-class and not pretending to be anything else,' said Felipe, harassed.

'Just look at him.'

On the court the tall rangy figure was now waiting for the blond boy to serve. Dancing from foot to foot, he exuded energy and effortless coordination.

'Upstart,' finished the older Señora Montijo with venom.

'Mama, he's a great guy,' protested Felipe. 'Came up from nothing. He's educated himself. Now he's putting half a dozen brothers and sisters through college as well, I'm told. And I've seen for myself that he's got a great business brain.'

Rosa Montijo shuddered. 'And how did he get the money to start this business? Can you tell me that?'

Her daughter-in-law took a hand. 'You know perfectly well, Mama,' she said indignantly. 'He won it. All right, he hasn't won any of the big titles. But he's won plenty of prize money during his career.' She cast a harassed glance at their visitor. 'You mustn't give Abby the impression that Emilio is some sort of criminal.'

Felipe said soothingly, 'You didn't mean that, did you, Mama? Seriously, Abby, you needn't worry about meeting undesirable types here. One of the business magazines did an article on him a couple of months ago. He must be a millionaire by now. He never had to—'

'Look,' interrupted the matriarch. 'Now! Tell me that isn't showing off. Go on, look!'

They all looked.

Emilio Diz dealt briskly with a workmanlike serve. The blond put the full force of his arm into his return. Even from the terrace they could see the way the dark man's expression changed. Suddenly he was glittering with triumph. Then he was running backwards, lithe and sure-footed. The ball soared over the net, high and hard. Emilio Diz jumped, reaching. His body arced like a dolphin. In flight it was clear that the tanned limbs were pure muscle.

'Look at *that*,' said Annaluisa, forgetting her hostess manners in simple awe.

Rosa Montijo sniffed. 'Gypsy. He's just trying to pretend he's more than a millionaire. At Bruno's expense.'

There was a crack like the report of a gun. A shout of triumph rose from the throats of two dozen watchers.

'He doesn't have to pretend, Mama,' said Felipe dryly, joining in the applause.

The game was over. The two men were shaking hands over the net.

'He could have given Bruno a chance,' said the resentful grandmother. 'He is your guest, after all.'

'You don't understand Emilio, Mama,' said Felipe.

The dark tennis player strode off the court. He was swinging his racquet as if impatient to get at the next challenge.

The spectators gathered round Bruno, punching him on the back, shaking hands. But Abby, watching, saw that they were more careful of Emilio Diz. Or maybe they were just more respectful. They gave him a drink. They talked. But they didn't touch him, those tactile, relaxed people who touched everyone.

A confident redhead approached and batted her eyelashes at him. He looked amused and didn't walk away. But Abby had the impression that he *would* walk away the moment he wanted to, gorgeous redhead or no.

Felipe confirmed the feeling. He had taken off his sunglasses and was watching the dark star intently. 'He doesn't give anyone special treatment. Emilio plays to win,' he said. He sounded just a little afraid.

The afternoon party turned into a barbecue, as they so often did.

'Do you want to borrow a dress, Abby?' said Rosanna Montijo, trying hard. 'We'll be dancing afterward.'

'Do you think I need to?' asked Abby, trying in her turn.

'You'd probably feel more comfortable. Well, I would in your place. The run up to Christmas is not exactly formal but the parties are, you know, sort of special. And anyway, people expect to dress up for Montijo parties.'

Which Abby interpreted as, 'For heaven's sake, don't turn up looking like a schoolgirl again and let us all down.' She suppressed a sigh.

'Then, thanks. Yes, please.'

Rosanna took her off to her room and Abby tried hard to enjoy the dressing-up session with Rosanna and her two best friends. They tried to include her in the conversation. But she did not know any of the boys they were talking about. And the tactics they discussed made her go hot with sympathetic imaginary embarrassment.

Then she heard a name she knew.

'Is Emilio staying for the dance, Rosanita?' said one of the friends, playing with her hair in front of Rosanna's crowded dressing table.

Rosanna was inside her walk-in closet. She poked her head out of the door. 'Yes.' She added in naughty Spanish, 'He struggled but Papa told him he had to stay and meet the right people.'

Abby translated the words in her head and nearly laughed aloud. She knew exactly how the tennis player felt. Maybe he was bad at mingling, too.

'That means he's the guest of honour, Abby,' said the friend, translating kindly.

She did not need to translate. Abby had prepared for this

trip by applying herself hard to Spanish. If she had to learn a new language, she thought, it might just as well be one where there were audio tapes available. But ever since she arrived, all the Montijos and their friends had brushed aside her halting attempts to speak their language. Abby did not know whether that was because they were too courteous or too impatient to let her fumble. But it had depleted her small store of confidence even further.

Rosanna emerged with a long burgundy dress. It was a sophisticated colour, too sophisticated for a sixteen-year-old, Abby thought at once. But they insisted that she try it on. So she did.

It swirled nicely round her legs when she moved. Only then they insisted on her borrowing some high, strappy shoes and she did not dare to move any more.

'I'll fall off,' she said, hanging on to bedpost.

'Not if you practise. You can't wear kitten heels with a dress like that,' said Rosanna fairly.

Abby tried to say that she did not want to wear the dress, either. There was a lot more wrong with it than the too subtle colour. It was more low cut than anything she had ever worn in her life. It made her feel uncomfortable. She said so. Rosanna gave her a shimmery scarf to wear with it but could barely hide her impatience.

'Honestly, Abby, I don't see the problem. It's summer here, for heaven's sake. Everyone wears low necklines in the summer. No one will even notice.'

'I'll notice,' said Abby, dragging the designer fabric higher over her small breasts.

A bootlace strap slid off her shoulder. She hauled it back. The front of the dress slid back to its former anchorage. She grabbed it with both hands. In the long mirror she looked flushed and stubborn and acutely uncomfortable.

'Well, you can't wear a T-shirt and shorts to a party,' snapped Rosanna, losing patience. 'Not in Argentina. Your father,' she added, clinching it, 'would really mind.'

The others agreed. They turned a deaf ear to Abby's reservations about the shoes, the straps, the sheer backlessness of the dress. They had done their best for her and now there were more interesting things to discuss.

'My father says he's going to go a long way,' said the friend at the dressing table.

The one painting her nails shrugged. 'Who cares? He's gorgeous *now*.'

Abby was in no doubt who they were talking about.

'My grandmother's terrified he'll seduce me.' That was Rosanna in her underwear, inspecting her smooth legs.

The others hooted. 'Fat chance.'

'Wish he'd seduce *me*.'

'He's got his own fan club, you know. My sister told me that in Paris last year, the girls followed him everywhere. Once even got into his bedroom at the hotel.'

They all paused to consider the prospect, sighing enviously.

'Well, tonight,' said Rosanna with decision, 'he's going to seduce me or no one.'

They teased her.

'In your dreams.'

'How are you going to manage that?'

'I shall tell Papa,' announced Rosanna superbly. 'He wants Emilio to meet the right people? Fine. I've known the right people since I was born. I shall take him round and introduce him to everyone here. And then,' her eyes went brooding, 'he can thank me properly.'

They all giggled.

Abby eased out of the door.

Nobody noticed.

So later, as twilight began to fall and more guests arrived, Abby went out into the famous gardens and tried hard to lose herself behind a tree. It was not difficult. Rosanna had too many friends to greet to spend time making sure that Abby circulated. The young people went to the paddock where the great barbecue was alight, while the older, glamorous crowd went up to the house.

The columned veranda glittered with diamonds and champagne and the tinkle of sophisticated laughter. No refuge with the older Montijos tonight then. Abby sighed and clutched the glamorous scarf round her as if it was a granny shawl. Oh, well, there had to be somewhere in the extensive grounds where she could take refuge. She slid away.

From his place on the terrace, Emilio Diz watched the girl with detached interest. She was not much more than a child. Not a Montijo, he thought. Not with clothes that fitted that badly. Her long arms and legs seemed out of her control, like a newly hatched crane fly. But she certainly knew what she wanted. She kept smiling and nodding to groups as she passed, but he could see that she did not let anyone delay her progress.

Where was she heading with such determination? He speculated idly. Maybe she was going skinny-dipping in the creek Felipe Montijo had told him about. But no, he shook his head at the thought. You didn't go skinny-dipping on a warm summer night alone, not even if you were still at the crane fly stage.

Oh, God, he was so bored, he was making up stories about a teenager he did not even know. With an effort, he brought his attention back to the group of businessmen he had been invited to meet. They wanted to meet him and they wouldn't for long. His celebrity was already on the wane. He had to capitalise on it before it died. He had a family to provide for, a growing family after Isabel's bombshell.

At the thought of his sister's news, his mouth tightened. Isabel was not much older that that little crane fly girl. Maybe if he had been home more when she was as young as that girl out there, she would not be in the terrible mess she was now.

Still, there was nothing he could do about that. All he could do was use his talents to provide for them the best way he could. Talents and contacts, he reminded himself, turning to look at his host's hundred best friends. Designer dresses and diamonds, even at a barbecue. And they had all known each other all their lives.

Make the most of it, he told himself dryly. If you don't bring this deal off, you won't be asked again. These people wouldn't have had you past the gate three years ago. And they won't again if you don't make it. Listen and learn!

CHAPTER TWO

ABBY had found the rose grotto at the Hacienda Montijo almost by accident. It had been planted by a Montijo groom for a romantic bride who was missing Europe badly. The design owed more to illustrated fairy books than any classical garden. The bride, taken aback, had not had the heart to tell him that the rose beds at Versailles were neither so crowded nor so cobwebby. Soon enough, she had a baby and stopped missing her old home altogether. But the rose grotto was established and Montijos held on to what they owned. Gardeners pruned and weeded and replanted, even though the family never came there.

To Abby it was heaven. Not as tangly and scented as the overgrown roses at home, of course. This garden was still properly cared for by professionals. But it was still recognisably natural. She sometimes thought that it was the only thing in this place that was, apart from the horses.

Now she tucked herself onto a mossy stone seat and leaned back, inhaling the evening scents. Content at last, she felt her tense shoulders relax. Immediately both borrowed shoulder straps fell down her arms.

'Blast, bother and blow,' said Abby peacefully and left them there. There was, thank God, no one to see.

She tipped her head back, dreaming...

Emilio did not like champagne. It was the first thing he discovered after he won his first big tournament. The second thing was that it was impossible to sign all the autographs they wanted and hold a glass at the same time. The third was that, like it or not, able to write or not, you took a glass and you pretended to drink because that was what made the sponsors feel comfortable. And if they felt comfortable with you, they forgot you weren't one of them.

Not that he wanted to be one of them. But he wanted to do business with them. And this year was crucial if his ten year game plan was to work. In fact, this *evening* was probably crucial.

So why was he so restless that he could hardly bear to listen to Felipe Montijo's important guests? Why did he want to vault over the balustrade and follow the crane fly girl in her escape? Opportunity did not knock twice. He had to seize it with both hands. *Concentrate,* he told himself.

He sipped the nasty stuff in his glass and bent his powerful attention on what his companion was saying about international wheat prices. The man was too polished to ask him for his autograph but Emilio recognised the look in his eyes, the curiosity about a celebrity. Well, he was a celebrity, for the moment. He had better be grateful and damn well make it work for him. He knew, none better, that it wouldn't last.

So he circulated, doing oil, bank software, and the prospects for the Argentine wine industry in the process. He gave out business cards and got rather more back. He stored the information for sifting tomorrow, giving thanks for his clear head and computer-accurate memory.

Then his hostess summoned them all to sit at tables set out around the lawn. Tall flambeaux had been driven into the ground and, now that the sun was gone, they were lit. A band set up its music in front of the tennis court. There was laughter from the paddock where the barbecue meats were being cooked. Some of the younger crowd appeared on the lawn and began to dance. Not the crane fly girl, though, Emilio saw.

He wondered where she was. Not chasing one of these callous young studs, he thought, conveniently forgetting that he was only a year older than Bruno Montijo. Emilio had been head of the household since long before his international tennis career started. He had never had anyone to mop up his mistakes for him, like golden Bruno.

Now he thought: someone should make sure that the little crane fly was not deceived by Bruno or one of his cronies. These romantic summer nights, it was all too easy.

He glanced round the tables casually. Bruno was not among the dancers, he saw. Nor was Miguel Santana, another high-octane, low-conscience charmer that Isabel had been out on the town with. Or several others.

Emilio hesitated. But no one was paying any attention to him for the moment. And he had more than done his duty by his ten year plan. He stopped hesitating and escaped.

He found the creek easily enough. There was a pretty circle of trees by a small dock. He could imagine people diving off it. But this evening it was deserted. The younger Montijos were either still eating or had started to dance.

Where was she?

He could not have said why he was searching for her. He told himself that it was because she looked uncertain, another stranger in the Montijos' magnificent midst. Being a stranger had its dangers. Maybe she didn't know the creek. Maybe she could have fallen in and needed rescuing.

But it was not that and he knew it. Maybe it was that she looked as out of place as he was. Only in his case it did not show on the outside.

Or maybe it was because Isabel had been an uncertain stranger and nobody had rescued her.

Abby was utterly peaceful for the first time in days. She could hear the soft lap-lap of the creek, beyond the hedge of honey-tinged albas. The darkening sky was splashed with lemon and apricot at the horizon but the impatient stars were out already. In this wonderful clear air, they seemed so close, you could stretch up and touch them if you could bother to bestir yourself. And all around her was the scent of the roses.

They were not roses she knew. There was a peppery pink

and a deep, deep crimson that smelled like hot wine. As for the palomino coloured climbing rose that surged around her stone seat—she reached up and buried her nose in it. What did it smell of? Abby shut her eyes. Concentrating.

Emilio found the grotto by accident. At first he thought it was just a gardener's corner, hedged around to hide tools and a compost heap. But a perverse desire to see the decaying cabbage leaves of elegant Hacienda Montijo pushed him through the break in the hedge.

To find what he had not admitted he was looking for! He stopped dead.

She did not notice him at first, his crane fly girl. She had her nose buried in a big tatty rose. Its petals were the colour of French toast and its leaves were almost black. As he looked she raised her head and, eyes closed, inhaled luxuriously. Her oversophisticated dress was nearly falling off. But she was oblivious to everything but her rose.

'Paper,' she said aloud. 'No—parchment. And something else. Cloves?'

She opened her eyes and bent to take another connoisseur's sniff. She never got there. She saw him. Her eyes widened in dismay.

Well, at least she wasn't going to ask him for his autograph, thought Emilio, trying to be amused. But he was not. That look piqued him. His time had not yet passed. People were still eager to welcome this celebrity. He did not like being toadied to, of course he didn't, but he wasn't used to people glaring at him as if he was an evil destroyer from another planet, either.

He nearly said so. But at the last moment he changed tack and decided to use the legendary charm instead. If it worked on journalists and crowned heads, who saw a lot of world-class charm, it ought to work on this odd creature in her ill-fitting dress.

'Sorry, I didn't mean to disturb you,' he said with the crooked, rueful smile that the photographers loved.

It did not appear to work. Emilio was taken aback.

The girl frowned mightily. It looked fierce. But of course she must be having to translate in her head, he thought, suddenly understanding the significance of the words he had overheard. Now was she American? Canadian? Australian? English?

He said forgivingly, 'I'll go,' and waited for her to tell him to stay.

She stood up and said with great care, 'I thought I am—sorry, I thought I *was* alone.'

All right, she wasn't going to tell him to stay. But she probably did not have the vocabulary for it. He recognised the wooden accent.

'English?' said Emilio in that language, strolling in to the centre of the bower.

She looked annoyed. 'Yes. But I try to speak Spanish. I did a course before I came out here specially. Only no one will *let* me.'

He selected another rose from the torrent and lifted it on one long finger.

'That's probably because your ideas are too interesting to get lost in first-grade vocabulary.' He tried another smile. 'What was it you said this thing smelled of? Parchment?'

She nodded seriously.

'And what does parchment smell like?'

To his amusement she closed her eyes to answer him with total attention. 'Linen. Dust. Afternoon sunshine through tall windows onto a stone floor. Maybe a touch of beeswax.'

He blinked, startled.

She opened her eyes and saw it. It was her turn to be amused.

'I know my smells. And I know my roses.'

'So I see.' He let the rose fall back among its brothers and looked at her curiously. 'Isn't that an odd hobby for someone your age? How old are you, as a matter of interest?'

Abby sighed. 'Sixteen. And age has nothing to do with it. It's not a hobby, it's necessity.'

He sank onto the grass at her feet and looped his arms round his knees.

'Explain,' he commanded.

Abby looked down at him, taken aback. No man had ever sat at her feet before. Oh, her brothers sprawled all over the place. But they never actually sat and studied her, dark eyes intent, as if they had nothing in the world that interested them except her and what she had to say.

In spite of the evening breeze that stirred the roses, she suddenly felt uncomfortably hot.

He laughed softly. Abby pulled herself together.

'Our garden,' she said practically, ignoring the heat she could feel behind her ears. 'It's planted with all the old roses. But there's no one but me to look after it. I learned which was which because people wrote letters about them and someone had to answer.'

His eyes were very dark brown, like the mahogany table in the big dining room at home, only when it was buffed so that it shone like glass. That had only happened a couple of times in Abby's memory but she remembered it vividly. It turned the table halfway to a mirror, so that everything looked different. It was the same effect of this man's strange eyes. Even in the twilight she could see the way they glittered. It was not comfortable.

The long, curling eyelashes did nothing to soften their expression, either. He looked as if he knew exactly what effect that melting expression had. As their eyes met, his mouth lifted in a half smile.

That made it worse. Abby raised her chin.

'So tell me—' His voice was like a lion's purr, deep and languorous. Deceptively languorous. This was not, thought Abby, a creature you would want to lull you to sleep. 'If I wrote to you about your roses, what would you tell me?'

Abby met his eyes and found they were like a caress. The

warmth was palpable. Instinctively she turned towards it, like a flower to the sun. She could almost feel her skin being stroked.

She brought herself up short. Caress? Stroked? What was it her father had said? She thought that people always meant what they said and she had to learn that they didn't?

Learn, she told herself feverishly. *Learn.* Whatever it feels like, it's not real. No glamorous man wastes caressing glances on a scrubby teenager unless he has some ulterior and probably unkind motive.

No, she definitely didn't want him lulling her into anything. She took refuge in briskness.

'That we don't sell plants. You can have a leaflet about the old roses. You can go on the waiting list to come to one of the summer open days. That's it.'

'Where does the leaflet come from?'

Abby grinned. The grin lit up her face, making her briefly beautiful. She did not know that, of course. 'Me mainly.'

He stared at her for an unnerving moment. But in the end all he said was, 'What's it about?'

Abby laughed aloud. 'Rose of Castile, introduced by the Crusaders in the twelfth century, red, pink or white with occasional stripes. Very strong fragrance. I think it smells like Turkish Delight but some people think that's unkind. The White Rose of York, of course. White with golden stamens. Another strong pong, less headachy than the Rose of Castile. Sweetbriar. Pink. True rose scent. The leaves smell like apples.' She ran out of breath and sent him a naughty challenging look. 'Shall I go on?'

'You're clearly an expert.' He sounded slightly put out.

Well, at least he had stopped looking languorous. Though that was a two-edged sword, because he stood up and she saw how the muscles bunched and relaxed in the graceful movement. Abby could not remember ever noticing the way a man's muscles rippled before and she lived in a house in which it was virtually impossible to avoid them. She flushed again, hating her transparent skin.

He said abruptly, 'Who did you come with? I didn't see you earlier, did I?'

'I'm staying here. This afternoon I was with Señora Montijo watching the tennis...' She made a discovery. 'You're that tennis player,' she said, without thinking. 'The one who beat Bruno.'

Briefly his eyes flashed. 'Oh, you're a friend of Bruno's, are you?'

'No. I've only seen him from a distance. In fact his grand-mother was annoyed with me for not recognizing him when you were playing him, I think. The house is full of photographs of him and I should have known which was which. Especially as—' Realisation hit her. 'You're Emilio Diz. You're *famous.*'

How right she had been to resist that caressing look. Not just a glamorous man but the guest of honour! An international tennis star who according to Felipe Montijo had been dating movie stars for years! And she had nearly let him lull her into—well, into—she was not quite sure what. She knew she was blushing furiously.

Emilio saw the fierce colour rise and said goodbye to any more untainted conversation.

So this was where the little crane fly asked for his auto-graph, after all. He sighed inwardly. Well, as long as it was only his autograph. Too many teenage groupies wanted a kiss. Or more. The incident in Paris had left a scar. He braced himself to be kind but firm

He misjudged her.

'You shouldn't be here talking to me,' said Abby, so ag-itated that she leaped to her feet, to the imminent danger of decency, as the straps of her dress fell further. 'You should be mingling. They wanted you to meet— I mean, you're *important.*'

Emilio laughed aloud. 'Not that important.'

He reached out and twitched her straps back into place, one after the other. It was a passionless gesture, almost absent. He might have been tidying a younger sister. But Abby was suddenly breathless.

His hand fell. His eyes grew intent.

She said hurriedly, at random, before he said anything she couldn't deal with, 'I know that Señor Montijo wants you to meet some people.'

He took a step forward. 'Met them.' He did not sound as if he could be bothered to think about it further.

'But you're the guest of honour, aren't you?'

He flung back his head and gave a great laugh at that. It revealed a long tanned throat. He was as strong and beautiful as the horses in the Montijo stables. And about as tame, thought Abby, shivering with a nervousness she only half understood.

'Guest of honour?' said Emilio Diz scornfully. 'Is that what you think I am?'

'Th-that's what they said,' said Abby faintly. She did not want to remember what else Rosanna and her friend had said about him, in case she started blushing again.

'Then let me put you straight. As far as the Montijos and their kind are concerned, I'm a commodity.'

She didn't understand.

His eyes glittered. 'I'm a guy from the wrong side of town and I always will be. I have no advantages except an ability to hit a ball over a net at a hundred miles an hour plus. That gets my photograph in the papers. That's what they like. When the papers find someone else, the Montijos won't even remember my name.'

It was what the Montijo matriarch had said, too, so it must be right.

'Oh.'

Abby knew she ought to feel sympathy for him. Maybe even indignation. But she was shaken by these new little tremors and she could not think about anything except that golden skin under his crisp white shirt. About how his muscles moved like some great cat's, lithe and powerful and potentially deadly. About how easy it would be to slip her hands inside—

Fortunately he was not a mind reader.

'I shall do business with Felipe Montijo. Maybe even with some of the other men here tonight. Eventually. I'm on my way up and they can be useful. I have a family to educate.'

A family? A *family*? This golden puma of a man was *married*?

Quite suddenly Abby's trembling stopped as if she had been unplugged from a power source.

'But I am not a performing monkey,' said Emilio Diz, not noticing. 'I'll talk to who I want.'

'Well, don't waste your time with me.' It came out much more rudely than she meant. She didn't mean to be rude at all. But quite suddenly she was desperate to get away from this scented nightmare. 'I haven't had anything to eat. I ought to go to the barbecue.'

His eyes narrowed.

'You circulate,' said Abby. She was fighting a desire to cry, which was ludicrous. She hadn't cried once in all this horrible week. 'I'll get some dinner.'

But he wasn't letting her go so easily.

'We'll both get some.'

He took her back to the party, skirting the band and the dancers on the lawn. She could feel people watching them. Some with interest. Some with envy. Some—heaven help her—with amusement. She stumbled on the grass and he put an arm round her.

'Sit here. I'll get you a plate.'

Biting her lip, she perched on the fallen tree stump he indicated.

A waiter—these people had a *waiter* at a *barbecue?*—gave her a glass of something. Abby took it but didn't drink. She was shivering. She did not want to drink. She wanted to *run*.

But Emilio Diz was coming back with plates and forks, followed by a couple of men bearing the most enormous tray of meat Abby had ever seen in her life.

And quite suddenly she was the envy of every woman in the place. She could feel the air change around her. He gave her that caressing smile again, the one that started in his eyes and slid straight down her spine. And everyone looked. That slid down her spine, too.

So Abby had to smile and say thank-you and pray her dress would stay up.

She drank.

'Choose what you want,' he said, handing her the plate and beckoning the man bearing the tray to her side. 'I know the English like their meat rare.'

He picked up an instrument that looked like a toy devil's pitchfork and turned a couple of substantial steaks over. He speared a particularly red one and held it up for her inspection.

Abby shuddered. She drained the rest of the champagne and put her glass down.

'N-no thank you. I'm not that hungry. Perhaps some chicken?'

He put back the steak and gave her what looked like half a chicken.

'What else? Filet steak? Sirloin? Lamb?'

'No, th-that's fine,' said Abby, recoiling.

A group of dancers had broken off and came over. One of them was Rosanna. She looked at Abby's plate with concern.

'Are you feeling all right, Abby?'

'Abby,' said Emilio Diz softly.

Abby felt he had speared her with that pitchfork. She looked up at him quickly, shocked. Their eyes locked.

How could a man who was married look at her like that? Look at anyone like that?

The group did not notice.

'You need some meat,' said the voluptuous beauty who had been painting her nails in Rosanna's bedroom.

'I've got some.'

'No, no. *Meat*.'

'On an Argentine *estancia*, chicken and pork do not count as meat,' explained Emilio, amused.

'Of course not. Beef is what you need. Wonderful Argentine steak and wonderful Argentine red wine. Strength,' breathed Rosanna's friend sexily, 'and passion.' She was looking at Emilio as if she would like to eat him, too, thought Abby.

He looked even more amused. Amused, maybe just a little wary—and appreciative.

I don't understand these people, thought Abby in despair. How can that woman pant over him like that, quite openly, when he has a family? His poor wife must be at home waiting for him right now.

'Do you tango, Emilio?' murmured Rosanna's friend.

It did not, thought Abby, sound as if she was talking about a dance. Is *this* what Pops means about learning to hear what people mean, not what they say? She's not asking him anything. She's telling him she's available.

The realisation stabbed like a stiletto. Abby could feel herself getting stiffer by the minute. She was turning back into the English schoolgirl they all dreaded, in spite of the sexy dress. She nibbled a piece of chicken, trying to pretend she was at ease. She felt it would choke her. So she chewed hard, smiling.

'Of course,' Emilio said calmly.

Rosanna's friend licked her lips. Definitely wanting to eat him, thought Abby, repelled and fascinated in equal measure.

'But not,' he went on softly, 'in the open air, to a Paraguayan band, at a family barbecue.'

So he wasn't talking about a dance, either. Abby thought her heart would break. Which was crazy.

And then he did something which really did break her heart.

He took the plate away from her. Put it down on the grass with her discarded wine and took her hand.

Smiling straight down into her eyes he said, 'No tango. But come and hop about the Paraguayan way.'

Abby went. She could feel all the eyes burning into her exposed back. She clutched the glittery scarf round her like a security blanket.

He took her among the dancers and put his arms round her. His hands were powerful, experienced and utterly indifferent. It made no difference. Abby was as tense as a board.

'Relax,' he said, smiling down at her.

'I don't know how to do this dance,' she muttered. She knew she sounded sulky. She couldn't help it. Oh, would this evening never end?

'Listen to the music and trust me. All you have to do is march in time. Just put a bit of a hop into it as you land.'

She did. It worked. She forgot her wretchedness for a moment, looking up at him with a grin of pure triumph.

His hands tightened. Suddenly she thought he was not so indifferent after all.

One of the other dancers, an older woman with kind eyes, spoke as she jigged sedately past.

'You've got the bachelor of the evening there, Abby. Don't hang on to him too long. You might get lynched. You're too young to die.'

It was a warning. Veiled. Kindly meant. But a warning none the less. Emilio knew it. His mouth tightened as he looked down at her.

But the warning went straight past Abby. All she could think was: *bachelor?* And then she remembered the conversation between the Montijo women. Emilio was putting his brothers and sisters through college? Something like that?

So the family he had spoken of did not include the wife she had imagined sitting at home waiting for him.

'Thank you,' she said. To the woman, who had danced

away. To Emilio, guiding her through the dance, with a hold that even unsophisticated Abby knew was a little too tight.

She tipped her head back and looked straight into his eyes. And smiled, dazzlingly.

It was quite dark now. The flambeaux illuminated the party but there were plenty of shadows if you wanted them. Emilio, it seemed, wanted them. He danced her out of the light.

'Careful,' he murmured. 'There are a lot of people out there watching.'

He was trying to sound cool but his breathing was uneven. Abby could have hugged herself.

'So?' she said naughtily.

What she did then was utterly out of character. Maybe it was the unaccustomed champagne she had drunk too fast, suddenly catching up with her. Maybe it was the night, the stars, the music. Maybe it was because she had danced for a good ten minutes with a man who actually wanted to dance with her. She hadn't actually felled anyone or fallen off her high heels, either. Both were firsts.

Or maybe it was, quite simply, the man himself.

But in the darkness Abby leaned into him.

He went very still.

Oh, Lord, he had brought this on himself, thought Emilio. Why had he not seen what he was doing? She was so young, his little crane fly. So innocent. He had not thought—

It was going to be like Paris, all over again. Only with the daughter of one of Felipe Montijo's influential business contacts.

Great stuff, Emilio! He congratulated himself silently. Just what you need to start the new career off with a bang.

More important, it was just what little Abby did not need, with the Montijo girl and her cronies circling like vultures. His sister had taught him just how cruel teenage girls could be.

He had thought he was doing her a favour by dancing her out of the spotlight. But it seemed he was leading her into something worse. Now, how was he going to stop her making a fool of herself? She would never forgive herself.

Abby stood on tiptoe, and brought his head down to meet her kiss.

Hell, thought Emilio.

Her mouth tasted of the wine but her skin smelled of flowers; those roses she had talked about, perhaps. She did not know how to kiss and she was quivering like a newborn colt. His heart turned over. This was dangerous!

He caught hold of her hands and held them away from him, not gently.

'I think not.'

Abby could not believe it. He sounded so casual, so indifferent. Yet for a moment—surely?—his mouth had moved under hers. Or had she imagined it?

It was as if he had driven that little silver pitchfork right in under the third rib. For a moment Abby literally could not breathe.

Wanted to dance with her? Who was she fooling? Men did not *want* to dance with plain, awkward schoolgirls who broke things and fell over their own high heels, not for pleasure. He was being kind. Kind like Rosanna and Señora Montijo. Kind like her father.

They all knew she was a disaster. They all tried to help. They all failed.

She wrenched her hands out of his hold. And then, of course, the inevitable happened. The thing that had been threatening all evening. The danger she had skirted so closely ever since Emilio found her among the roses.

The borrowed dress fell off.

Well, it fell to her waist. For a moment she was so busy flapping her hands free that she did not notice.

He muttered something which her Spanish was not advanced enough to interpret.

And then she realised that the cool breeze was cooler than it should have been. She looked down.

Emilio was fighting his baser self with every weapon he

knew. In the starlight her skin looked silvery. The small breasts were exquisite, so gently rounded, so softly firm. She looked like a cool water nymph. But she was warm and her flesh smelled of roses. His head swam.

'This is not fair,' he said under his breath, half laughing, half in despair.

He wanted her so badly it hurt.

Abby did not see it. In fact Abby was not seeing anything very clearly through her fog of shame and rejection.

She grabbed at the dress. At the same time, she took an unwary step. There was nothing she could do. She was already off balance. Those killer shoes only completed her downfall.

She tried to recover, to step back from him. But it was too late. Her ankle went over. She lurched, arms flailing.

And fell into his arms.

For an electrifying moment, she was crushed against him. She felt the heat of his body against her shivering; the smooth slide of the shirt against her aroused skin.

And then—

And then—

Somehow he found the strength.

'Careful,' Emilio said.

He steadied her with easy competence. His hands were utterly kind. Utterly impersonal. He did not know how he managed. His heart felt as if it was in a vice and his whole body was on a knife edge. But he did it.

For Abby, it was the final humiliation.

She kicked the hateful sandals viciously. The impetus sent the second one spiralling up high, high, so high that for a crazy moment it was outlined against the starry sky.

And he laughed. He *laughed*.

'Great shot,' Emilio said, with amused admiration. Sophisticated admiration.

It was more than she could bear.

Abby fled.

CHAPTER THREE

THERE were three girls in the trendy ladies' room of Culp and Christopher Public Relations. The tall brunette was painting on eyeliner carefully, pulling a horrible face as she did so. The tall blonde was observing the operation critically.

'Don't squint, Abby. You'll lose the line.'

And the tall bottled redhead was sitting with her booted feet on a marble tabletop, reading aloud from a pile of newspapers.

'Listen to this,' she said. '"The Fab Ab turned me down. Boy band heartthrob Deor Spiro, 22, said, 'I just wasn't good enough for her. I will never love again'. See pages 4, 5, 9, 10 and 11. Our Tracy says, 'The girl has everything. Why should she tie herself down?' What do you think? Ring the number below and tell us.'"' She lowered the paper. 'Wow, Abby. Your own poll, no less. How did you do it?'

'I didn't,' said Abby. The words were muffled because her tongue was stuck firmly between her teeth as she concentrated. She was still not very good at eyeliner. She finished the job, lifted the tiny brush carefully and stopped grimacing. Recapping the gold tube, she said over her shoulder. 'It was all done by heartthrob Deor Spiro, 22. And his publicist.' She added dispassionately, 'Little toad.'

'He may be a little toad,' said Molly di Perretti, pushing aside that newspaper and reaching for the next, 'but what did you do to him?'

'Squashed him flat, I bet,' said Sam Smith. She flicked back her blond hair and met Abby's eyes in the mirror. 'Am I right or am I right?'

Abby shuffled her fashionable shoes uncomfortably. 'Well,

he wouldn't take no for an answer. It was like talking to someone who didn't speak my language.'

'He's a man,' said Molly, cynical to her black-and-silver fingernails. 'They don't engage brain when they're in coming-on-to-you mode.'

'Careful,' warned Sam. 'Abby's got all those lovely brothers. She thinks men are great.'

Molly did not blink. 'I think men are great. I just don't expect to *talk* to them.'

'Well, I do,' said Abby with spirit.

'That must have shaken heartthrob Deor Spiro, 22,' Molly murmured irrepressibly.

Abby gave her sudden wide grin. 'It did. I don't think he'd been turned down before.'

'Oh, he'd been turned down, all right' said Sam. 'Many times over the last fifteen years.' She was ten years older than the other two and spoke with authority of a successful career in the public relations.

Abby did the arithmetic. 'You mean he's not twenty-two.'

'Nearer thirty-five if you ask me. But it's wonderful what tan stick and a puppyish manner will do for a man.'

'To say nothing of blond highlights and a photographer who's an airbrush artist,' said Molly, surveying a portrait in the next paper critically. 'Hey, this is a good one, Abby. "The It Girl With Taste." Love that.'

Abby put her head on one side, surveying her image in the mirror.

'Taste?' she said doubtfully.

The other two exchanged looks of fond exasperation.

'You look amazing, Ab,' Sam assured her.

Abigail Templeton Burke did a little jig in front of the full-length mirror. It was an experimental jig. When Abby turned into Abigail Templeton Burke, socialite and PR person, she sometimes did not feel quite like herself. It took a mirror and waving her long legs around to remind her.

Mind you, at least these days she could stand upright on

high heels, she thought. It had taken her time to get used to it. At home she strode around in trainers or boots most of the time. Wearing heels was second nature to her now but it was a skill she had largely learned in this very cloakroom.

Now she turned to the side to inspect herself.

'Yup,' she said without vanity. 'But would you call it tasteful?'

Tall and broad-shouldered as a model, she wore her clothes well. Today it was silky black pants that flopped around her four-inch heels as she walked. The square of black silk she wore over her breasts to complement the trousers was only turned into a garment by the shoelaces criss-crossing her tanned back.

Molly lounged to her feet and joined Sam in circling round her. They considered the outfit with critical professionalism. Dressing the part was a requirement of the job at Culp and Christopher Public Relations. Finding the right gear to hit the catwalk shows of the London Fashion Week had not been easy.

'Tasteful, schmasteful,' pronounced Molly. 'It will do the business. That's a real lust bucket of a top.'

Sam took longer to make up her mind.

'Brilliant,' said she at last, on a long breath. Her sigh was at least three-quarters relief. Left to herself, Abby had a tendency to dress as if she was just about to go out to the stables. She said so.

'Give me a break.' Abby was not offended. 'Up to six months ago that was exactly what I would have been doing.'

They knew it. The other girls in the agency were even sympathetic, against all the odds. They decided to take Abby in hand almost as soon as she arrived in the PR consultancy. As a result, today's look was the result of group consultation. It had involved half the office and at least one up-and-coming designer.

'Maybe not brilliant,' Abby demurred now. Her golden-brown eyes twinkled. 'Ravi said I needed to make more of a *statement*.' She wafted her hands through the air in a very good imitation of the languid designer.

The others laughed. But Sam said soberly, 'You stay just as you are now. Any more of a statement and you'll be putting the client in the shade.'

'In your dreams.' said Abby cheerfully. Glancing back at the mirror, she pushed a hand through her soft dark hair and thrust out a hip, posing. After a moment, she shook her head regretfully and straightened.

'Nah. Diane Ladrot's safe. Nice enough but dull. No competition there.'

She said it without regret. She had had boyfriends. They did not last and when they went their way, Abby was almost relieved. Perhaps it was spending so long in the comparative isolation of the country. Perhaps it was because she instinctively responded to men the way she did to her brothers. But one way and another she had never seemed to get the hang of dating. Looking at the disasters that the other girls at C&C went through, she was secretly not too anxious to try.

No doubt it would happen at some point. When it did, she would do her best. But she was certainly not looking to set up in competition to Diane Ladrot or any other man magnet. Abby did not regret her lack of pulling power.

The other two exchanged glances. They knew she believed it. Abby had absolutely no idea of her own appeal. Or that, if she put her mind to it, she could have been quite as stunning as their most glamorous client.

Originally the staff at Culp and Christopher had greeted the appointment of the Earl of Nunnington's only daughter with dismay. 'Another deb mucking about so she can get her name in the papers,' was the general consensus. But Lady Abigail, though inexperienced and appallingly unstylish, had neither mucked about nor shown any desire at all to feature in the gossip columns of the national daily papers. It had taken a great deal of concerted work by her new friends to get the sort of coverage that she was picking up today.

Not that Abby was aware of it, as both Sam and Molly knew. She thought it was chance, and did not take much notice of it. She did not realise that the agency found it very useful to have a girl on the strength that the press were already interested in. Abby, though, thought her job was exactly the same as anyone else's at the agency. She worked hard and did her fair share of the dull stuff.

Indeed, Molly, her closest friend at the agency, sometimes thought that the dull stuff was what Abby preferred.

Take today, for instance. For anyone else, accompanying a Hollywood film star to fashion shows would have been a rare and welcome perk. Sure, there was a job to do. You had to make sure that the client got maximum coverage from whichever media turned up. But the shows were buzzy and exciting.

As Molly herself said, it beat sitting on the phone for hours trying to persuade world-weary radio editors in Scunthorpe to run your story. But Abby didn't see it like that. In fact, Molly had the distinct impression that to Abby it was a chore—and not a very welcome one.

Which was odd, given the way she looked now that Ravi Kamasarian had done his bit.

'You could give Diane all the competition she could handle if you wanted to,' Sam said flatly. 'Thank God, you don't.'

'It's a shame, really,' Molly said now. 'Bit of sparkle and that outfit could be really glamorous. But Sam's right. Best not.'

Abby turned away from the mirror without sparing her reflection another glance. 'Just as long as I fit in.' She flexed her shoulders under the criss-crossing.

'You'll be cold though,' said Sam, ever practical.

Abby shrugged. 'Oh, these shows are always overheated.'

Sam and Molly exchanged looks.

'You've been before?'

It seemed unlikely, given her attitude to clothes. But they

were constantly disconcerted to discover the things unsophisticated Abby turned out to have done without them having any noticeable affect on her life skills.

Abby had a wide, mobile mouth. When she wanted she could make a clown's face. She did so now.

'You'd be amazed at what I'll do for charity,' she said with a grin. 'At least, what I used to do.' The grin faded a bit.

There was an uncomfortable silence. Abigail had never been disloyal. She never mentioned her family in any way. But it did not take a mathematical genius to calculate that the time between her father's spur of the moment wedding and Abigail's departure from the Palladian mansion in which she had been her father's hostess since she was twelve, was a matter of days. Just about enough time for the newlyweds to get back from their luxury safari and the new Lady Nunnington to turn her stepdaughter out of doors, in fact.

So, Abigail Templeton Burke, aged twenty-five and untrained except in the running of thirty-room houses and organising the social life of a jet-setting aristocrat businessman, had suddenly come on the market. Culp and Christopher reckoned themselves lucky to be the first in the race to get her title, her contacts and her cheerful common sense. Abby reckoned herself lucky to get a job.

Now Sam said, 'Do you think there's any chance of you getting back for the meeting with Traynors this afternoon?'

That balanced common sense would come in really useful on this one, Sam reflected. To say nothing of the soothing effect of the title on a bunch of a nouveau riche property developers.

Molly looked wise. 'Think it's going to be sticky, Sam?'

'I'd put money on it. Traynors have been getting terrible publicity for weeks. It wasn't great to begin with. But then they got into this take-over battle and there's been real mudslinging. Not our fault, but heck, who's counting? Now they've been bought up, the old management will be doing everything they can to hang on to their jobs.'

'So?' said Abby, frowning.

Molly and Sam exchanged glances.

'Management is a macho game,' explained Molly kindly. 'You lose, you're out. So the guys who ran it before it was bought up will be trying to demonstrate to the guys who are their new bosses what hard men they are.'

'That means they'll need to do two things,' said Sam from the depths of her experience. 'Sack someone. Preferably with maximum publicity. And shift the blame for anything that went wrong onto someone else. I see the buck whizzing rapidly in this direction.'

'They'll blame us?' said Abby. 'But that's not fair.'

'You're learning,' agreed Molly. 'Corporate life isn't fair. It's a game without rules and all that matters is winning.'

Abby shivered. 'Nasty.'

'Yup. Short of a miracle, Culp and Christopher are going to take the blame for this one. And lose the account,' said Molly philosophically. 'That why you want Abby, Sam?'

Sam gave a rueful laugh. 'You are so right. I foresee a real shouting match before the clients sack us. If you're there, it might take some of the steam out of the meeting. They don't know you, so they can't shout at you.'

'Besides, people never do shout at Abby,' said Molly, grinning.

'I know. It's like having a security blanket. If you can make it, I could really do with you, Abby,' Sam said, with feeling.

Abby was touched.

'I'll try,' she said obligingly. 'Depends on the latest version of Diane's schedule. Still, perhaps she'll want a rest, with the premiere this evening.'

'More likely the film company will be running journalists in and out of her suite at ten minute intervals,' said Sam, depressed.

The new film was her project and she was not getting on very well with the film's publicist. There had been a number of clashes on the stars' timetables but Diane Ladrot's was the worst because she wanted to take in the London Fashion Week shows as well.

'She'll have to have her hair done at some point,' Abby said consolingly. 'I'll see if I can make a run for it then. What time's your meeting?'

'Three. But it will go on for ages,' said Sam with gloomy certainty.

'Well I'll get back as soon as I can. I'll slide in quietly,' promised Abby. 'No one will notice I haven't been there all the time.'

It was fortunate she could not see how wide of the mark that airy forecast would turn out to be.

Emilio Diz said, 'I will attend this meeting.'

He put the cap on his pen as if there was no more to be said. The Gypsy-dark face was quite expressionless.

The dignified squabble that had broken out between the finance director and the head of marketing immediately ceased. The board of Traynor Property Development looked at each other, unified at last in their dismay.

'Come to the PR company?' echoed the head of marketing hollowly.

The managing director thought on his feet. That was why he was still managing director, ten days after the Diz Corporation had acquired Traynor in a ruthlessly effective take-over.

'But you said your first priority was to see what we had in development, Señor Diz,' he reminded Emilio smoothly. 'I've organised a tour of our current sites.'

Emilio looked at him for an unnerving moment. The managing director felt the hairs on the back of his neck rise though he could not have said why. There was nothing to be read in the soot-black eyes.

'I toured the sites before I made a bid for this company,' Emilio said coolly.

The managing director was shocked. No one should have been able to gain access to work sites without authorisation and everyone at the table knew it.

'I don't understand,' he said stiffly.

'It's quite simple.' Emilio allowed himself a grim smile. 'I always do my research. Your security is garbage. Put the two together and—' He shrugged.

The managing director had nothing to say.

Emilio nodded, as if he expected to silence his subordinates and this small victory was no surprise. As indeed it was not.

'So I will attend this meeting,' he concluded.

No one had told the marketing director that you did not argue with Emilio Diz. 'But why?' he said, genuinely puzzled.

'Because this company's public relations stink,' Emilio said brutally. 'Before I can put it right, I need to find out whose fault it is. Yours or the agency's.'

That was too much for the young finance director. 'What about a hostile bidder's mud-slinging?' he burst out.

The black eyes rested on him with even less expression than before, if that was possible. There was a sharp silence. Everyone round the table held their breath.

Then—'Quite,' said Emilio coolly. 'I was *seriously* unimpressed by your defence. Almost made me withdraw the bid.'

There was a concerted gasp. He ignored it.

'So I'll lead the meeting with Culp and Christopher at three.'

His voice said that was the end of the argument. Everyone recognised it.

The fashion show started an hour late. That was par for the course. Abby expected it and used the time well. Diane

Ladrot had a few gracious words with the daytime TV news crew, chatted for longer with a reporter from an influential London radio station and had her photograph taken by every paparazzo present.

'Good work,' she said to Abby, slipping into the seat reserved for her in the front row. 'That felt real easy. Very casual. Just what the punters like. You're good at this, aren't you?'

'So are you,' said Abby with respect.

The film star pulled a face. 'I'll be ragged by tonight, though. Have you looked at the programme?'

Abby was sympathetic. 'Do you want to skip the next show?'

Diane sighed. 'I want to skip the whole damn afternoon.' A thought occurred to her. 'You know, maybe that's not such a bad idea.'

But Abby was distracted. She had just caught sight of the last person she wanted to see.

It was a horrible shock. She could not believe it. What on earth was Justine doing here? She was supposed to be in Yorkshire, waiting for her husband to come home from his travels.

Abby bit her lip. What on earth was she going to do? Every instinct urged her to look hard in the opposite direction and pray that Justine didn't see her. It was cowardly, she knew. But she had no idea what to say to a stepmother who openly disliked her.

She was still frowning over the problem when the music throbbed into life. The lights swung into action and the first models sashayed down the catwalk. Abby sank back and tried to concentrate on the clothes.

Afterwards, Diane wanted to place an order. Abby waited for her, not looking at the third row where her stepmother had been sitting. The room emptied fast as people stampeded for the next prestige show.

Justine would have gone with them, Abby assured herself.

She would not be late for a high fashion event. Especially not just to exchange words with her unwanted stepdaughter.

But Abby was wrong.

'There you are,' Justine said behind her. It was the tone she dreaded. Sharp and cold and critical, even when there was nothing to criticise. 'I didn't expect to see you here. Does that job of yours give you time off to go to fashion shows?'

Abby felt herself freeze at the naked dislike. It was a sensation she had never felt until six months ago. Now she was all too familiar with it.

She turned slowly, taking deep careful breaths. 'Hello, Justine,' she said quietly. 'I'm here for my job.'

'Oh.' Justine's purple-painted mouth thinned with discontent. 'Doing what?'

'With a client,' said Abby uninformatively.

It was her job to protect Diane from unwanted contact with fans, as much as it was to make sure the star got maximum media exposure. Justine, as Abby had found out painfully, was avid to meet celebrities. The problem was, she could not be relied on to be civilised when she did.

'Which client?'

But Diane answered that herself, emerging from the curtained changing area with the beaming designer. Justine's eyes popped at the Hollywood star. With the premiere of her new film set for tonight, Diane's postered image was on every hoarding in London.

Justine took a step forward.

Mindful of her duty and Diane's punishing schedule, Abby interposed her shoulder before Justine could advance.

'Sorry, no time.'

Justine glared at her. Except when Abby's father was there, Justine did not bother to disguise her hostility.

'You think you're so clever, don't you?'

'No,' said Abby. She could not say anything else. She had no time and anyway the pit of her stomach was making threatening noises. She was beginning to feel sick, as she always did after a few minutes of Justine's company.

'Everyone thinks butter wouldn't melt in your mouth.' Spite made Justine's eyes gleam. 'But I know better. You just battened off your poor father until I put a stop to it.'

This was so far from the truth that Abby was not even hurt. Even nauseous as she was, she laughed in Justine's face. And forgot that she had promised herself not to answer Justine back.

'I was the best unpaid secretary Dad ever had.'

'Unpaid!' Justine's voice rose to a screech.

Across the room even the designer, absorbed in her starry client, looked up, startled.

Justine took a step forward and stuck her face up towards Abby. Her head jerked backwards and forwards like an angry goose pecking at an intruder. It was somehow both ridiculous and frightening, thought Abby, recoiling.

'You're a parasite. Your father has never stopped paying you off. Even now,' Justine hissed.

'Now?' Abby was blank.

'Any normal girl would have found herself some friends to share a flat with. A man of her own. But not you. You're going to cling on under his roof until someone kicks you out, aren't you?'

Abby sighed. 'If this is about the garden flat...'

When his children were still at school, Lord Nunnington bought a family home in a garden square just south of the river. As they left university and moved through various careers and relationships, all the boys had made their home there at some time or another. Lord Nunnington, who hated London, spent as little time there as possible, preferring to head straight for his Yorkshire home when he returned from his international trips.

So when Abby came to London, he had said, 'Better take over the garden flat.' And she had.

Justine had made it clear from the start that she resented it. Now she said cruelly, 'Any *normal* girl would want her independence.'

'I am independent...'

'And privacy.'

'I have my own front door. My own living quarters, my own kitchen. That is privacy.'

Justine ignored that. 'When I was your age, I couldn't have borne to live under my father's nose. Girls ought to have somewhere to take their friends back without their parents knowing every move.'

Abby set her teeth. Justine had needled her on this subject before.

'If by friends you mean boyfriends, why don't you say so?' Abby said crisply

Justine gave her a pitying smile. It did not reach her eyes.

'All right. If you don't mind, why should I?' She sighed elaborately. 'That's why I thought it would be so good for you to come to London.'

Abby was politely incredulous.

Justine's smile slipped. 'Well, you'll never get a boyfriend if you carry on like you did in Yorkshire. You dress like your grandmother. You even behave as if you're ninety.'

Abby stared. She felt more and more sick. This was ridiculous, she thought. But ridiculous or not, it was frighteningly nasty.

Justine could have read her mind. Quite suddenly, she lost all vestige of control. Abby had seen it before and flinched. That seemed to infuriate Justine even more.

'Don't think you can look down on me, you lumbering lamppost,' she spat. 'If no one else will give you your marching orders, I will.'

The malice was naked. Abby stood her ground but only just.

'Oh, please,' she said in distaste.

She turned away.

'Don't turn your back on me,' screeched Justine.

She was now thoroughly enraged. There were two little red spots on her cheekbones. They did not coincide with her careful blusher. It made her look like a witch.

But she did not seem to care or even to know. They were

attracting an interested audience of the designer, her assistants and Diane Ladrot. But Justine did not seem to notice them, either. She hauled Abby back round to face her with a scarlet-painted claw. The Nunnington diamond and several ornate rings weighed it down.

In a last desperate attempt to avert the unforgivable, Abby said brusquely, 'I haven't got time for this. I've got a job to do.'

'Job! Huh!'

'It's how I earn my living.'

'Earn! You don't earn one damn thing and never have. You wouldn't even have a job if your father hadn't pulled strings.'

Abby whitened.

Justine saw she had struck home at last.

'If you had any pride, you'd get out of our house and stand on your own two feet.'

It was then that Abby lashed back at last. Fatally.

'You mean like you do?' she suggested with poisonous sweetness.

Their eyes locked.

Plenty of people had speculated on Lord Nunnington's hasty marriage. But no one had called Justine a gold digger to her face before. In particular his children, well brought up and very fond of him, had been meticulously polite, no matter how hard Justine pushed them. To find that Abby was not as dumbly docile as she appeared was a shock to Justine. Ugly colour rose, swamping her expensively imported make-up.

Her mouth snapped tight as a trap. 'I want you out,' she said between clenched teeth. 'Today.'

She dashed off, leaving Abby more shaken than she wanted to admit.

After that Abby did not find it easy to concentrate on the job in hand. Oh, she got Diane to successive fashion shows and then back to her hotel. But she was only listening with half an ear to the star's conversation.

Your father pulled strings... Dress like your grandmother... They echoed in her head. *Behave as if you're ninety...*

But then she remembered what she had said herself. She had more or less accused Justine of marrying her father for his money. Justine was never going to forget that. Still less forgive. What was more, she was quite capable of telling Abby's father unless Abby did what she wanted.

And back came that last, cruellest cut.

I want you out. Today.

She would have to leave the garden flat. But how could she manage it today? Justine would have to give her a few days to sort herself out. Surely she would do that, Abby told herself. Not with much conviction.

'You've not heard a word, have you?' said Diane, with more tolerance than might have been expected from a world-famous star.

Abby jumped. 'Sorry,' she apologised.

'No sweat. That woman with the rings really upset you, huh?'

'Yes,' Abby admitted. She pulled herself together. 'But that's no reason for not doing my job. Let me—'

But Diane was interested. 'What did she say?'

That I'm out on the street.

No she couldn't say that. Abby picked one at random.

'Dress like your grandmother?' echoed Diane, amused. She surveyed the silky top under Abby's trim jacket and grinned. 'You must have had a hell of a grandmother.'

Abby smiled gratefully. 'This is just dress up for today,' she admitted.

'OK. So you need a bit more permanent razzmatazz. That can be arranged.' A naughty glint came in to Diane's eyes. 'In fact, that might fit in very well.'

She pushed aside her plate of salad and leaned forward confidentially.

'Now, here's my idea...'

CHAPTER FOUR

SO FAR Emilio was not impressed by Culp and Christopher. He did not like the expensive premises, the tortured artwork in the foyer or the clipped English voices which thought they were so superior. Above all, he hated the titles on the staff. He knew all about that sort of snobbery and it infuriated him. Did they think he was going to pay them good money for shoddy work, just so that he could say Lady Abigail Wotsit was working for him?

No one would have known from his contained demeanour that he was furious though. He sat down, read his presentation folder and took notes just as if he was really considering renewing the agency's contract. It was a sham.

There was no way this bunch of incompetents was going to get a new contract out of Traynor, Emilio promised himself. The agenda they had set out for the meeting was way off the point. The chief account officer, fair-haired Englishman wearing a purple silk shirt and too much cologne, waffled for forty minutes without saying anything. And half the Culp and Christopher agency's account team had not even bothered to turn up.

Emilio turned his folder round for one last glance at the papers they had prepared. Then he took charge.

'I think,' he said crisply, 'that I have heard enough.'

It took the purple silk shirt some time to wind down. Emilio did not even pretend to listen. He was reviewing the notes he had made during the first forty minutes of the meeting. There were not enough of them. Proof, if he needed it, of the high waffle to substance content.

'We are here to establish only two things,' he said now.

51

'Where Traynor's negative publicity came from. And how we turn it around.'

The purple silk shirt, who had been listing the press releases he had issued and the media attention he had attracted, started again.

Emilio shut him up him with a look. 'I'm not querying the work you've done. I'm asking why it has had zero effect.'

There was a nasty little silence.

At this unpropitious moment Abby opened the door. Every single eye turned. So when she tried to slide into the room unnoticed, it was hopeless. She might as well have brought her own spotlight.

Not, thought Sam Smith, shaken, that she would have stayed unnoticed for long anyway. For since her departure this morning Abby had undergone a transformation. Oh, she was still wearing her stylish black trousers and jacket. She probably still had the shoelace-backed top on underneath but fortunately it did not show under the conservative jacket. It was not her tanned back that set jaws dropping It was her *hair!*

The hair was Diane's brilliant idea. 'I need a rest,' she had told the celebrity hair dresser when he came to her suite. 'I'll wear the stylist's dress but I don't want my hair changed. Just give me a wash and blow dry later. But as you're here, will you please help my assistant,' waving a hand at Abby. 'She wants,' she added naughtily, 'some permanent razzmatazz to liven up her boring life.'

So Abby returned to Culp and Christopher with her soft dark hair transformed into haystack spikes of turquoise, streaked with rich plum.

Emilio looked at her and his eyes widened. Just for a moment and totally out of character, he forgot what he was saying. He stared. So did everyone else; but he did not notice that.

The girl looked as if she was going to a party. No, it was worse than that. She looked as if she had just got in from a party. A wild party. He had been to parties like that himself when he was on the tennis circuit.

Emilio frowned. There had been a time, before he set up his business, when he had partied as hard as any of them. It was not a memory he wanted to recall in the middle of a business meeting.

Well, that settled it! The moment he walked in he knew this damned firm was pretentious. The meeting had demonstrated that it was incompetent. Now a member of their staff wandered into the meeting late, looking as if she would be happier in a nightclub. Incompetent, pretentious and covering it up with phoney glamour. How on earth could Traynor ever have thought they would get a serious job out of Culp and Christopher?

He closed his briefing folder decisively.

The purple silk shirt came out of his trance with a jump.

'Oh Lady Abigail. You're back.'

Lady Abigail! It was the last straw.

Emilio's eyes glittered dangerously. He stood up. The others followed suit.

'Let me introduce the newest member of our team,' said the account office quickly before Emilio could march out of the door. 'Lady Abigail Templeton Burke.'

There was a dangerous moment when Emilio did absolutely nothing at all. His eyes narrowed to slits. Everyone held their breath.

Then he gave a short nod.

'Lady Abigail,' he said curtly.

Abby was unnerved to find everyone looking at her. It distracted her briefly from her own problems.

'Er—sorry I'm late.'

It did not occur to Emilio that her clipped voice was the result of nerves. Still less did he detect shyness. To him it sounded like the last word in upper-class indifference. For once, his face was not expressionless.

Abby felt that familiar lurch of the stomach. Oh, no, not

twice in one day, she thought. That was just not fair. Justine
had been bad enough, but this dark man glaring at her for no
reason at all was more than she would put up with.
Unconsciously, her chin tilted.

He looked absolutely thunderous, thought Sam Smith,
alarmed. Fighting mad and dangerous with it. She began to
realise why the Traynor's team were looking shell-shocked.
And Abby was eyeballing the man as if she was about to go
twenty rounds with him!

Hurriedly Sam pulled out the seat next to her and hauled
Abby into it. She slid a briefing folder in front of her and
hissed, 'Read! This is sticky!'

Abby bent her head obediently over several pages of Day-
Glo slogans. She hardly saw them. That momentary locking
of glances had shaken her. Though she would never have
admitted it for a second, she was still vibrating.

Emilio smouldered. Women did not defy him and then
ignore him! Never had done. Certainly didn't these days; not
now that his wealth could move mountains. But the tall girl
with the turquoise hair was doing just that. She even shuffled
the briefing sheets as if she had just dismissed him from her
mind. Slowly he sank back into his seat.

The Traynor's team watched him nearly as anxiously as
Culp and Christopher. He was oblivious. He did not take his
eyes off Abby.

'Have we interrupted your day, Lady Abigail?'

Hitherto, his English had been perfect Mid-Atlantic in
phrase and tone. Now suddenly the husky voice was heavy
with Spanish consonants. Why did a Latin accent always
sound so threatening? thought Sam.

Abby raised her head as if she had been shot.

Sam could see that the girl was struggling not to quail.
That was when she realised that Abby, exceptionally, was
wearing quite heavy make-up. And under it she was pale.
She wished suddenly that she had not asked Abby to join the
meeting.

Abby was fighting back though. She pulled herself together and gave him one of her pleasant smiles. 'No.'

'You're sure?'

Abby felt as if she was on one of those moving floors at funfairs. You thought you'd got yourself standing upright and the damned thing slipped sideways again. This was actually much nastier than Justine. This man, whoever he was, had no right to harangue her like a machine gun. For some reason, he set all her nerves jangling as if she already knew him. And had reason to fear him.

Yet she did not. Well, all right, he looked vaguely familiar but that could be what he was wearing. Eighty per cent of the men who came in here wore conservative city suits. His voice was a different matter. That felt even more so familiar, somehow. Was he a movie actor of some kind? But what would a movie actor be doing scaring Traynor's tigerish management into panic?

She leafed through her papers again and again but his name wasn't on the list of visitors. She had never met him before, that was why Sam asked her along, so there would be a stranger that the hostile forces had to be nice to. And now he was yelling at her, the one person who was supposed to bring some calm to the proceedings. It wasn't *fair*.

'I've apologised for being late,' she pointed out crisply. 'You're not the only client, you know.'

The purple silk shirt shut his eyes in anguish.

Emilio was taken aback.

Sam Smith leaped into the breach. 'But this raises an important point. We've done a bit of work on it but, frankly, most of the adverse exposure hit us unawares. If you turn to sheet number five, you'll see our analysis....'

Even Emilio Diz turned to sheet number five eventually, though he took longer about it than anyone else. He seemed reluctant to take his eyes off Abby. Abby herself, speed-reading a completely new client history, seemed unaware of that brooding regard.

She worked hard at seeming unaware. She would have been pleased if she had known how totally she succeeded. *Oh, Lord,* thought Sam looking at Emilio Diz. She was a student of human nature and she foresaw fireworks.

She was wrong.

Certainly the discussion became heated. But Emilio, sitting back, took no part in it. He was watching the interplay between Traynor's and the PR agency's team, with only the occasional flicker in the direction of the bent head of Lady Abigail. So far, it was pretty much as he could have forecast; each side trying to blame the other: neither side looking at the real issues. He sighed and was about to take charge again when a mobile telephone began to ring.

Emilio frowned mightily. All the Traynor team checked their phones guiltily. But no, they were all switched off as he had commanded. The ringing continued.

'*Abby,*' hissed the account executive.

Emilio went so still he might have been turned to stone.

She jumped and came out of the folder.

'Is it yours?'

She rummaged in the loose pocket of her jacket and brought out a phone as tiny as a powder compact. She was aware of Emilio watching glacially as she opened it and tapped acceptance. She put it to her ear.

'*No,*' moaned the executive.

But Abby was listening with total concentration, her eyebrows knit.

She turned away from the table. 'I can't talk now,' she said in a low voice.

In vain. Everyone in the room was listening.

Emilio watched her. He saw her mobile mouth thin to a fierce line.

'No,' she said, clipped and cold to freezing point.

Who was it? thought Emilio, intrigued in spite of himself. An angry lover? He could only see her profile but she looked shocked. More than shocked, he realised suddenly. Hurt. Yes, that was it. She looked so hurt that she was not capable of disguising it, even in this room crowded with strangers.

Emilio found himself thinking: whoever he is, the man on the phone is making more impact on her than I have.

But what about the impact I made nine years ago? Is this the girl who kissed me with such innocent passion in the Montijo's garden? The one I managed to resist? And have never ceased regretting resisting!

It was unlikely of course. It would be an amazing coincidence. After all, he had only talked to her once, all those years ago, and she had only just been struggling out of adolescence. Would he trust himself to recognise her again? All he knew about her was that she was English and called Abby.

He watched the girl's jaw clench suddenly, as if she had expected suffering but not this much. Surely only someone she was passionate about could make her look like that? The idea of Lady Abigail passionate was something else that intrigued him.

Maybe she was his Abby after all.

'I apologise, gentlemen,' said the account executive. 'Abby, please go outside if you must take the call...'

Abby nodded. She said into the phone, 'Yes, I understand. I've got to go.'

Whatever the caller said made her whiten, suddenly and alarmingly. Well, no one else seemed alarmed, Emilio realised. He was surprised. To him it looked as if all the blood had drained out of her, in spite of the ski slope tan. He did not like her but if he had been closer, he might have been tempted to put an arm round her to steady her.

Abby's jaw was rigid. 'Don't worry. I will.' She shut the phone with a snap and pressed the off switch. 'Sorry,' she said turning back the table.

That last remark sounded more like a threat than a promise, thought Emilio. He was more and more intrigued. Maybe the lover was on his way out? He found himself speculating idly on what sort of man Lady Abigail would take as a lover.

Speculating so profoundly, that he missed several of the next exchanges. Missed everything, in fact, until Abby herself joined the discussion.

It cost her a lot to transfer her attention back to the meeting. She was, frankly, in a cold panic. Suddenly these bad-tempered clients did not seem to matter much in comparison, not just at the moment, anyway.

The phone call had been from Justine. Abby was wrong in thinking that Justine would give her time to find somewhere else to live. In her most vicious mood, she had called to deliver a deadline. An unmeetable deadline, as Abby well knew. She set her teeth and refused to think about it.

Concentrate, she told herself. *Concentrate!*

She absorbed the last of the folder's contents furiously. Then cast discretion to the winds and spoke her mind. 'I don't see how you can expect people to like you if you keep tearing down their favourite buildings,' she said clearly.

There was an audible gasp and everyone looked at Emilio. His eyes narrowed but he said nothing.

After a moment's hesitation, Traynor's managing director decided to be amused. 'That's supposed to be your job, isn't it?'

Abby, however, was frowning over the material in front of her.

'Public relations is supposed to be about getting people to recognise clients' names and associate them with positive values,' she recited. She had been taught it only a few months ago and it was fresh in her mind. 'But how can anyone get Traynor associated with positive values when you're deliberately telling people it doesn't matter what they think, you're going to do exactly what you want anyway?'

The managing director stopped being amused. 'Pro-gress—' he began.

'Maybe it is progress,' Abby allowed. 'Did you show any-one how your developments were going to make their lives better? Did you even think about it? Because if you did, you sure as hell never told us.'

Sam could not believe it. No one could believe it. Cheerful, peace-making Abby on the warpath?

Abby could hardly believe it herself. But the silence of the man at the head of the table spurred her on. If he was going to sit there smouldering at her, she was jolly well going to give him reason to smoulder.

She tossed her head. There was no familiar soft fall of hair against her cheek. The turquoise spikes made her feel naked. Not just the spiky hair, either. There was something about that man's eyes that made her feel as if she had forgotten to put on her clothes this morning.

She unfocused her eyes so she did not have to watch him smouldering. Or see her underlying nakedness reflected back at her.

She said hardily, 'People aren't stupid, you know. And PR doesn't do brain-washing. You want us to persuade people your new buildings are a good idea? Fine. Give us some evidence.'

The silent man's eyes had narrowed to slits of light. Steely light. Abby glanced at him quickly and looked away at once. She concentrated on the foaming managing director.

'Isn't that supposed to be *your* job?' she challenged him.

Sam could have groaned aloud. Where was the friendly Abby who took the heat out of every argument?

Emilio Diz closed his folder.

Oh, Lord, thought Abby, I've really done it now. He looks as if he wants to kill someone. Probably me. What got into to me?

But she knew what had got into her. It was being smouldered at. She didn't like it. So she had probably thrown away her embryo career because he rubbed her up the wrong way.

Brilliant, Abby, she told herself. Kiss the home and the career goodbye in a single day. She held her breath, waiting for the blow.

But, to her astonishment, the hateful man said, 'You have a point.' It sounded as if it strangled him to admit it. But at least he was not smouldering at her anymore.

Abby blinked. Everyone else at the table looked astounded. Sam sent up a silent prayer of thanks.

'I will consider further.' His Spanish Rs rolled horribly. 'I don't think we can do any more today. Let us close this meeting.'

The executive had expected to lose the Traynor account. He did not quite know what to do with this reprieve. Floundering, he said, 'Of course. Whatever you say. Er—' He pulled himself together. 'Why don't I give you a cup of tea in my office? Or a drink. Glass of wine, gentlemen. Then I'll walk you round. See the sort of operation we have here. Meet the staff...'

He fully expected Traynor's alarming new owner to crunch him. Instead Emilio Diz seemed to debate inwardly. It took less than ten seconds before he shrugged and accepted.

'Great,' said the account executive hollowly. 'This way.'

The Traynor's brigade trooped out behind their new general, accompanied by everyone but the women.

Left behind, Sam sagged.

'What happened?' she said. 'I thought you were going to bite him in the fleshy part of the leg.'

Abby was conscience stricken. 'I'm sorry. Only he just sat there sneering at us all, saying nothing...'

'Saying nothing?' Sam echoed. A look of comprehension crossed her face. 'I was talking about the managing director,' she said dryly. 'Not the seriously sexy article that has just taken over that bunch of cowboys.'

'Sexy?' echoed Abby. 'That human volcano?' She shuddered. 'Semi-human,' she corrected herself conscientiously.

'Well, *you* weren't looking at anyone else,' Sam pointed out.

'No but—' Abby caught herself. 'Yes, I was. I was reading the brief.'

'And nor was I,' Sam went on frankly, ignoring her protest. 'He's gorgeous.'

'He's nasty.'

'Well, yes, that, too. Most tycoons are.'

'Then they should learn some self-control,' said Abby coldly. She stood up. 'Can I go back to my own clients now?'

Sam stood up, too. 'I don't know what you're so mad about. He couldn't take his eyes off you.'

Abby looked angry. 'Because he didn't like me,' she said shrewdly. 'Me coming in late like that really made him mad. I suppose he expects people to be lined up and waiting when he arrives.'

'Well, he is paying for our time,' said Sam fairly.

'But I was doing him a favour. Traynors aren't my client, thank God.'

'He wasn't to know that.'

Abby shrugged. She didn't want to find anything to say in the smouldering volcano's defence. Her stepmother's call had knocked the bottom out of the world and she was feeling savage. It was a relief to find someone who deserved her fury.

She glanced at her watch. After six o'clock. She had been at work since seven-thirty. She could perfectly well have gone home.

Home? Abby gave a hollow laugh. And found it broke.

She dived for the ladies' room.

What a contrast with their cheerful chatter this morning, she thought. She let the tears fall for a while. Then she heard someone in the corridor outside and wiped her eyes hurriedly. Her unaccustomed make-up smudged horribly. She tried repairs but her hand kept slipping.

In the end, Abby gave up and washed it all off. Then she went back to her desk and banged through the pending box and the day's e-mail with Olympic energy. By the time she finished it was dark outside, the open-plan office was empty except for her. There were lights in a couple of the manage-

ment offices but Abby ignored them. Normally she would
have put her head round the door to say goodnight, see if
they wanted to share a coffee or a drink before they went
home. But tonight she was too sore. And, frankly, in too
much of a mess.

She did not know what to do. Of course she did not really
believe that Justine would have changed the locks on the door
to her flat. But pride made her determined not to go back to
the house tonight if she could help it. So she had to find
somewhere to stay. But where?

None of her brothers was in London. She could go to a
friend, maybe Molly di Perretti. But Molly had gone home
an hour ago. If Abby turned up on her doorstep unannounced,
she would have to explain that her stepmother had thrown
her out.

If she had been at home in Yorkshire, there would have
been dozens of friends she could go to. But—in London?
Abby did not yet know anyone well enough to trust them
with a secret like that. And she knew her media by now. She
knew it was too good a story for the gossip columnists to
resist if they got wind of it.

She went out into the agency's courtyard car park. There
were only a couple of cars left, discreetly dark and shining
in the rain. Abby felt a flicker of envy. It was going to be a
miserable walk to the tube, splashing through puddles and
trying to keep the rain from soaking through her smart jacket.
She opened her umbrella with savage jerks.

If the scandal only affected Justine, the columnists would
be welcome to print whatever they damned well liked, Abby
thought vengefully. But it did not. It affected her father, as
well.

She could not bear it if he found out from the papers that
open war had broken out between his wife and his daughter.
Once she had told him, then Justine could take her chances.
But until he returned from his current trip somewhere in up-

country Kazakhstan, Abby would do everything she could to keep the breach out of the papers.

Which meant that a hotel was not a good idea, either. She would have to pay with her credit card. The desk clerk would see her name. Desk clerks were a great source for news agencies. The last six months had taught Abby that much.

So she was stuck. Either she risked telling the world about her stepmother's viciousness. Or she went home and tried to talk herself back into a house where she did not want to spend another minute!

She did not realise that tears of temper and frustration were coursing down her cheeks until a voice said, 'Lady Abigail?'

She turned. It was the man who had smouldered at her. The big cheese who had just taken over Traynor. The smooth operator with the sinister accent. The man she had gone head-to-head with for the first time in her life.

Abby dashed the back of her gloved hand across her cheeks and hoped that he would think their dampness was due to the rain. Her chin tilted.

'What?' she said pugnaciously.

If she had batted wet eyelashes at him, Emilio would have nodded and gone his way. If she had smiled, he would have said goodnight and passed on. But he had spent a long, long hour with one eye on purple silk shirt's door waiting for her to come through it. And that glare was a challenge.

He hesitated. An irresistible challenge?

'Why didn't you join us?' he asked.

Abby groped for a handkerchief and failed to find one.

'Not needed,' she said curtly. She could not help herself. She sniffed, turning away impatiently.

For some reason, it touched Emilio. There was something oddly gallant about her belligerence. She had obviously been crying. But she was still fighting him with every breath she took.

Yes, the challenge was irresistible.

He said with practised charm, 'You're getting very wet. Can I offer you a lift somewhere, perhaps?'

As soon as he said it he was annoyed with himself. He had no time to go accepting challenges from turquoise-haired sirens. He had too much to do.

He was even more annoyed when he saw the undisguised alarm that flashed into her eyes. Did the wretched girl think he was making a pass at her, for God's sake? In a car park in the middle of an English downpour?

'A lift,' he repeated with emphasis. 'I was offering to take you home, no more.'

'Home,' she said in a strange voice.

Her psychedelic hair was dulled in the erratic light of the courtyard. But he had not forgotten that aggressive colour, to say nothing of the style. Maybe she went straight from her desk to the dance floor.

'Home,' he repeated grimly. 'Unless nightclubs open at,' he consulted his watch, 'eight o'clock in this strange country.' He was stiff with anger.

She gave a little laugh that broke in the middle.

'As of four-twenty this afternoon, I haven't got a home,' she told him in a light, hard voice.

Emilio did not know why, but he knew that it was the negligent tone that said it was true. He also knew that she was standing in the rain talking to him because she did not have the faintest idea what to do next. He took charge of the umbrella and drew her hand into the crook of his arm.

To his own astonishment he heard himself say, 'Then you'd better sit in the car and get dry while you think where you would like me to take you.'

Abby gaped. She had not expected the smouldering man to show kindness to anyone, least of all her. She was deeply suspicious. At the same time, she was half embarrassed, half desperate to comply. At least it would stop her thinking for a moment.

She compromised. 'Not your problem. Why should you help me?'

She resisted his urging to move towards one of the dark, warm cars. But she did not take her hand away from his arm.

'Problem solving is my speciality,' he told her, amused. 'That is how I made my millions.'

He said it casually but he was watching her narrowly to see how she reacted. It was a powerful word, *millions.* It changed the way people behaved to him. And it changed them in the twinkling of an eye.

Not Lady Abigail. She did not even notice the word, too preoccupied with her private struggle.

'This one isn't solvable,' Abby said soberly.

'We'll see.' But he sounded very confident. Even elated. Even to himself.

She gave up resisting and went with him to the car. He sounded so *certain,* she thought. And she was so very tired.

Idiot, she told herself. You don't need a man to tell you what to do. But it was heavenly to sit in the dry and relax for a moment. She tipped her head back against the leather headrest and closed her eyes.

Emilio got in beside her and surveyed her. Her nose tilted. Her damp eyelashes were long and silky. In spite of her ridiculous hair she did not seem to be wearing any make-up and her skin was soft and unblemished as a child's.

Was this that glowing girl who had lectured him on the scent of roses and then kissed him with her whole heart? Was it?

The internal light switched off automatically. Emilio drew a breath of relief. Against his will he was recalling, not the Montijo's garden, but those tennis circuit parties she had brought to mind earlier. There had been a time when he would have swept her off her feet and danced until dawn. Or until they fell into bed.

Hey! he thought, startled. You don't want to go to bed with Lady Abigail Wotsit. Do you?

Her eyes opened. In the shadows he saw the movement of those extravagant eyelashes. His mouth dried.

Do you?

He said at random, 'What happened at four-twenty to make you homeless?'

Then he remembered that one-sided phone call. At the time he had thought it was an angry lover. More than angry, by the sound of it. Who was he? And what had she done to make him throw her out?

And why did Emilio Diz waste even a moment of his precious time thinking about it?

She opened her eyes but she did not look at him. Staring straight ahead through the darkened windscreen, she said, 'It's complicated.'

She shifted her shoulders against the seat as if she were exhausted. A little eddy of her perfume reached him. His pulse accelerated. Just a little, but he recognised the feeling.

It was odd. He had not felt that little electric charge of sudden alertness for a long time. Attraction, yes. Sexual drive, yes. But not that sudden sitting up and taking notice when you didn't expect to. It intrigued him.

And then of course there was the matter of whether she was the girl he remembered....

'You had better let me buy you dinner while you talk me through it.' Emilio was amazed at how casual he sounded.

Oh, yes, he recognised it: pulse a little faster, senses a little heightened. Also, much more dangerously, head a little lighter.

Did she feel it, too? He could not read her expression in the car's dark interior.

'That's very kind.'

She sounded constrained. Because she did feel it, too? Or because she didn't?

'I don't think I should wish myself on a client, though,' Abby said.

Which answered the question neatly. If she felt it, too, she would not be thinking of him as a client. Just as well, Emilio thought. He had set himself a punishing work schedule for the next few months. There was really going to be no time for chasing women, even turquoise-haired party girls who shouldn't be too hard to catch. Except—

Except that she had made him angry, in a way that all Traynor's incompetent bullies had quite failed to do. Except that once he had let her go and never stopped wondering what would have happened if he hadn't. Except that she still figured in his dreams sometimes.

'You wouldn't be wishing yourself on me. You'd be doing me a favour.' He sounded amused, rueful, quite as if he didn't care whether she said yes or no. Emilio was proud of himself. 'Every dinner I've had in the last ten days has been on planes or with business partners. Or both. A real dinner with real conversation would make me feel human again.'

Abby hesitated. He could feel her hesitating. It was as if her whole body, even her breathing, had gone on hold.

How come I'm noticing her breathing already? thought Emilio, taken aback.

Then she gave an oddly shaken laugh.

'All right. Thank you.'

He felt as if he had won a great victory. He could have shouted with triumph.

Instead of which he put the car in gear and drove sedately out into the glimmering wet streets.

'Good.'

CHAPTER FIVE

'So WHERE did you live before you were homeless?' Emilio asked, easing the powerful car out through Culp and Christopher's decorative iron gates.

Abby tensed. This unknown client was probably not going to sell her secrets to the tabloid press if she confided in him. But there was no point in taking chances.

'Oh, south of the river,' she said vaguely.

'But in London?' he pressed.

'Oh, yes, London.'

Emilio frowned. His crane fly girl had definitely not been a London resident, with her garden of old roses that she was the only one left to look after. Perhaps he was wrong after all.

'And do you like living in London?'

If she had been telling the truth Abby would have said, 'No, I hate it. I feel as if I've been banished into exile. All I want to do is go home and never see this miserable, dirty, noisy, cruel place again.' But she was not telling the truth. She had not been telling the truth rather hard ever since her father turned up with Justine and announced that he was married at last.

So she said, 'It's cool.'

The dark client sent her a quick sideways look as if she had surprised him.

Abby had no idea why he shouldn't believe her. But she embellished her enthusiasm, anyway.

'Lots of places to go, people to see. At C&C they're saying that London's the hot city this year.'

'So you count yourself lucky to be here?'

'Yes,' said Abby firmly.

'But you're still homeless?'

That was a mean shot. Abby felt her heart lurch. She stopped emitting excitement as if he had pressed a switch to turn it off.

'Yes.'

'And you're in a panic about it.'

'No, of course not, I'm—'

That dark, disbelieving look again. She shuddered into silence.

Then she said carefully, 'What makes you think I'm in a panic?'

'Because you got into this car without asking my name.'

'*Oh!*'

'Unless you already know?'

She considered lying. She never used to be a liar but six months at Culp and Christopher had taught her the importance of giving clients the answer they wanted, especially when their ego was involved. A man with the millions he claimed would probably have the ego the size of the Empire State Building.

But then, she thought, this man doesn't sound as if he cares whether I know who he is or not. He does look vaguely familiar. But I can't place him. Anyway, there's no way I could keep up the pretence.

So in the end she said baldly, 'Haven't a clue.'

He gave a soft laugh. 'Well, it's all a long time ago. You would not have been much more than a child when I had my picture all over the sports pages.'

He was looking at her sideways again. Abby didn't like it.

She said crisply, 'Sport bores me, anyway. Who are you? Or should I say, who were you?'

'I am Emilio Diz. I *was* a tennis player on the international circuit. Fifth in the world for a while.'

'Oh? Congratulations. I don't know anything about tennis. That's my brothers' department. My brother Sandy was—'

And then it hit her. She had said this before. *I've heard*

*my brothers talk about him. They thought he would be
Wimbledon champion this year if he hadn't retired from the
circuit.*

It came back to her as clearly as if it was yesterday, not
nine years ago. The heat. The disapproving matriarch. The
duel on the sunlit tennis courts. And this man, fluid and
graceful as quicksilver and about as out of place.

She was remembering other words, as well. *You shouldn't
be here talking to me. You're important.* And not just words.

The night. The music. The dancing. Her first dance with a
man who wasn't just being kind, steering her round the floor
and trying to avoid major breakages. Her first dance with a
man whose arms she had wanted to be in.

Then, in the darkness, standing on tiptoe, bringing his head
down to meet her mouth. Her! Shy, awkward, ignorant Abby,
sixteen and terrified that people would find out how little she
knew, actually kissing a man of her own free will.

And the man holding her off.

The man who had held her off in her dreams ever since.
The man who had told her, finally and forever, that no man
would ever want her to kiss him in the shadows and mean
it. The man who had pulled the borrowed silk up over her
breasts and managed not to touch a millimetre of her skin.
The man who had *laughed*.

The man who still made her wince every time she thought
about him. How had she failed to recognize him?

'Oh, Lord,' said Abby, appalled.

So she *was* his crane fly girl. Emilio felt an odd fierce
triumph.

No one would have told it from his smooth voice.

'How do you do, Lady Abigail.'

'Er—how do you do,' muttered Abby, writhing inwardly.
She plaited her fingers in her lap. Did he know?

She glanced at him sideways. He was driving with easy
confidence, concentrating on the twists and halts of the busy

road. No, of course he didn't know. He probably didn't even remember.

How important could a simple kiss in the dark be? After nine years, too. Especially when it was a kiss he had rejected. He must have had so much practice at holding off starstruck teenagers in those days. He'd probably forgotten it before he had gone home that night. No, of course he didn't remember.

She said more easily, 'Is this your first visit to London, Señor Diz?'

'Emilio, please. No, I came every year when I played tennis. And recently, this has been a hot place to do business, too. In fact, I've just bought an apartment here.' He gave an amused sigh. 'And what a business that was. To say nothing of getting some furniture into it. Setting up home in London is no job for a busy bachelor. Still, it's done now. You must come and give me your opinion of it.'

Oh, he was all charm now that she wasn't a teenager anymore, thought Abby. It made her feel triumphant, but also forlorn. She wasn't so different from the awkward teenager, not inside. He wouldn't bother to turn on the charm if he knew what she was like inside.

She said, more tartly than she intended, 'My opinion wouldn't be worth much. I've never set foot in a millionaire's bachelor pad.'

As soon as she said it, Abby wished she hadn't. Would it offend him? Make him angry? He was an important client, after all. What was more, he had gone out of his way to help her when he could perfectly well have left her standing in the rain. He did not deserve her to spit at him like a bad-tempered kitten.

There was the pause of a heartbeat. The longest heartbeat Abby could remember.

'Then I look forward to giving you a new experience,' he said smooth as cream.

Abby stopped worrying about offending him. She sat bolt upright. Was the man laughing at her? *Again?*

But his tone was neutral when he said, 'In fact that may be the best place to go right now.'

'Why?' she said suspiciously.

He gave a soft laugh. 'Relax. I'm not going to kidnap you.'

'I didn't think you were,' said Abby furiously.

'Then you gave a pretty good imitation of it. But you needn't worry. I need to check on some things, that's all. We can stop off at the apartment and then go and find that meal. There are plenty of restaurants around the block.'

He paused. Abby said nothing.

'Or if you've changed your mind, I will take you anywhere else you want to go and we can forget dinner.'

Now she knew who he was, she would rather have had dinner with Count Dracula. Only of course she could not admit it. Anyway, there was nowhere she could think of to tell him to take her. And it was pouring with rain. And the car was so warm and comfortable.

Abby muttered, 'No. All right. I'll have dinner with you.'

'Thank you,' he said dryly.

Now that was *definitely* laughing at her. She retaliated in kind.

'You're welcome.'

He laughed aloud at that.

'Everything will look better when you've eaten. Now sit back and stop worrying.'

Slightly to her own surprise, Abby did.

She took the opportunity to look around her. In the intermittent light from the street she saw that this car was no millionaire's Lamborghini. It was discreetly dark, though the upholstery was leather and the dash gleamed with polished wood. Luxurious, powerful and completely anonymous, Abby thought. There was not so much as a map or a tube of sweets in the glove compartment to prove he was human. It was the car of a man who did not leave any clues. It was not a comforting thought.

No amount of understated luxury could hide the power of

the engine, though. As Emilio sent it surging along, Abby realised three things: Emilio Diz knew London well enough to drive a convoluted path through back streets that she had never seen before; that he handled the car with easy mastery; and that the nine-year-old attraction was still there.

The last thought scared her so much that she said the first thing that came into her head. 'Do you know where we are?' It sounded like an accusation, but she could not help that.

She was badly rattled and doing her damnedest to hide it. If he thought she was a back street driver, well tough. It was better than him thinking she was an overgrown groupie, sitting next to him with her tongue hanging out.

He glanced down at her. 'I always know where I am.'

'How comforting.' She was only slightly acid. He was trying to be helpful, after all, and she was getting her equilibrium back.

'Not comforting. Essential.' The accent was Mid-Atlantic again, amused, sophisticated and very nearly caressing. 'Like I said, I specialise in problem solving. The first rule before you can change anything is be quite clear where you stand.'

How could a voice make you feel as if you were being stroked? Abby shivered, half in pleasure, half wary. She had never come across a voice that affected her like this. No wonder her sixteen-year-old self had fallen for it so hard she lost all restraint. She suspected it was world-class seduction.

Determinedly she brought herself back to reality. 'That sounds like management speak,' she said. That was more waspish than she meant, too, but she could not do anything about that. Not if she was going to resist slipping under the spell of that voice. 'I mean, what does it mean—be quite clear where you stand?'

She found they were coming out opposite Green Park. He concentrated on turning the car into the stream of traffic. They went round Hyde Park Corner before he answered.

'It means know what you've got. Know what you want.

Above all, know what you're prepared to give up to achieve your goals.'

'That sounds very ruthless,' Abby said slowly. 'What about other people?'

'Everyone has to be responsible for himself. The secret is to know what things are worth in relative terms.'

She was thinking of her father. Had he taken a decision that his new wife was worth the loss of his family, if it came to it?

'And if some of the things you must be prepared to give up are people? Maybe they don't want you to give them up.'

He shrugged. 'We all have to move on.'

At least his voice was no longer caressing. Abby thought: he's said that before. How many times has he moved on? And what happened to the women he left behind?

She stopped the thought abruptly. She was shaken.

She had only met the man twice in her life, for heaven's sake. What was she doing thinking about the women he had left behind? They were nothing to do with her. *He* was nothing to do with her. An impromptu meal on a rainy night did not give him a place in the landscape of her life.

She grabbed for a change of subject and alighted on the luxury of the car.

'This car is so comfortable. What is it?'

He shrugged. 'I have no idea.'

Abby stared.

'It's a rental. I don't know whether I'll buy a car or not yet. I'm not sure how much time I'll be spending here. It may be easier just to rent.'

Abby was entertained. 'You'll spend all that money on an apartment but not buy a car?'

'An apartment is an investment. A car is a running cost,' Emilio said dispassionately.

She looked at him sideways. 'Yes, you are a typical businessman, aren't you? Most of the men I know would be much more interested in their wheels than a roof over their head.'

'It sounds as if the men you know need to grow up,' said Emilio with something of a snap. That crack about him being a typical businessman had hurt.

Abby tipped her head back. 'Oh, I don't know. A really swish car is a work of art.' There was real longing in her voice.

Against his will, he laughed. 'All right. I'll buy it. You drive a vintage Morgan, right?'

Abby sighed. 'I wish.'

He was genuinely intrigued. 'Then what?'

'Oh, I haven't got a car in London. At home I used to have a runabout. It was old but not old enough to call it vintage. It was always covered in mud which my father said held it together. No one but me would drive it because the gears jumped sometimes. I was the only who had the trick of it.'

She sounded wistful. Emilio registered it—and also that she did not seem to have any idea that her homesickness showed. But that's what it was. He knew all about homesickness. When he first went off round the world, as a junior, he had called the crowded shabby little house in Buenos Aires every chance he got. The others had laughed. But he had missed even the bad bits. Just as she did.

He said gently, 'What happened to this monster?'

'I'm not sure.'

He was surprised. He had her down as loyal, even to elderly and temperamental machines.

She said with constraint, 'I haven't seen it since I came to London. I suppose it may have gone for scrap by now.'

There was something badly wrong, thought Emilio. For a moment there she sounded almost on the edge of tears.

He ran through the information he had gathered so far. She had not been home to that place in the country with the old roses she did not know he knew about. She was not going to have a roof over her head tonight. She did not know what had happened to a car that sounded as if it was halfway to being a family pet. Yes, definitely something wrong. For all her turquoise hair and club land image, she sounded as devastated as his little crane fly had nine years ago.

Would she confide in him, though?

Yes, Emilio promised himself. Yes, he would get her to trust him if it took the whole evening. Work could wait. This was a girl in bad trouble.

He said, 'What would you like to eat? Indian? Thai? Italian?'

'Whatever you want.'

He was going through the back streets again. Abby was not as lost here as she had been in Mayfair. She had friends in Chelsea. It was full of tall white houses where she had been going to dinner before dances since she was fourteen. Emilio Diz, she realised, was as familiar with the area as she was.

'Have you lived round here long?'

He laughed. 'Two days.'

'I don't believe it.'

'I've known London forever. When I was younger I used to travel all the time. Never bought a house here before, though.' He was rueful suddenly. 'Not my best decision, so far.'

Abigail was intrigued. 'Why is that?'

'We're supposed to be talking about your problems, not mine,' he said, caressing again.

A rebuff, thought Abby. She was almost relieved. It tended to counteract the effect of that velvet voice.

They were in front of a red-brown Gothic building that she vaguely recognised. He turned into the underground car park. A uniformed man touched his cap as they swept in.

Abby saw a notice on the wall and made a discovery. 'This is the old hospital, isn't it? I read that they were turning it into luxury flats. What are they like?'

'Come up and see for yourself,' he said easily.

She hesitated for a microsecond. He picked it up, though. He was quick, she thought, unwillingly impressed.

'No strings,' he said dryly.

She stuck her nose in the air. 'I never thought there were.'

He parked the car and turned off the engine. The dark eyes glinted as he sent her a measuring look.

'Yes, you did. Very sensible of you, too. I'm sure your mother always told you not to go home with strange men.'

But for all the teasing tone, she knew he didn't like it. She didn't really blame him but she didn't know what to say. He frowned in preoccupation as he swung his briefcase out of the car. She followed him in the same silence.

She waited until they were in the lift. Then said carefully, 'My mother never told me anything. She died when I was twelve but she had been ill for years before that. My father did all the 'do not trust him gentle maiden' stuff. Not very well, poor darling.'

He was startled out of his reverie. 'What?'

Abby gave him an apologetic grin. 'Sorry if I was stupid back there. It's just that I'm not really a city girl and I don't always pick up the signals right.'

He looked at her hard for a moment. How could his eyes be so expressionless and yet feel like a laser beam? Abby looked back at him as openly as she could manage. It was not comfortable.

In the end he said indifferently, 'We all protect ourselves as best we can. I have no right to complain.'

He almost sounded as if he didn't care, too. Almost. But the Latin accent was back, Abby noticed. She was about to point it out when the lift stopped and he ushered her into his flat. She stopped dead.

It was empty. She had thought he was not a man to give clues about himself. But this was a totally blank canvas. Just acres of lemony-cream carpet and a fax machine on the floor in one corner.

'Good heavens,' she said blankly.

The drawing room was huge, with a tall window embrasure. The cushions on the window-seat were the only furnishings in the room.

Emilio flung his briefcase behind the door. 'I thought so,' he said grimly. He extracted his mobile phone and keyed in a number. 'Diz.'

Abby wandered to the window. Her boots left precise footprints in the deep carpet. It must be so new it had never been walked on before.

Behind her Emilio was talking to someone to whom he did not even bother to say hello. He rapped into the telephone, 'So what happened this time?' He listened for a few moments, visibly curbing his impatience. 'Let me get this clear. Your suppliers aren't able to deliver the furniture for ten days?'

If he talked to me in that tone of voice, I wouldn't answer back, I'd jump to attention, Abby thought.

The person on the other end seemed to have a less developed sense of self-preservation. The answer was extended.

Emilio's frown got blacker and blacker. Eventually the dark brows locked hard into a great fuzz of fury.

Oh, wow! thought Abby, backing away from the area of conflict.

'Fine,' he interrupted curtly. 'Cancel the order. I'll make other arrangements.' He snapped off the call before the person at the other end could reply.

Abby looked at him with trepidation. She did not really want to have dinner with a man seething with fury.

She need not have worried. With the end of the call, his temper seemed to disappear.

'Right,' he said pleasantly. 'Where would you like to eat?'

It was almost sinister, thought Abby, that total wiping away of all irritation. It was as if he was in absolute control of everything, even his feelings. All her misgivings started humming again.

If she had had someone to go to, she would have left then. But she hadn't.

'Wherever you like,' she muttered.

In the end he took her to a lively Italian bistro she had known all her life. Known well enough, at any rate, to be impressed by the effortless command which got them one of the two quiet tables in an alcove.

'Smooth,' said Abby, half amused, half uncertain. She only let the amusement show, though. 'These tables are like gold dust.'

He shrugged. 'The food is good but I don't like my conversation interrupted by amplified rock.'

For some reason she felt an urge to needle him. All that control was unnerving. The temptation to stir him up a bit was irresistible.

She raised her eyebrows. 'That's odd. You don't look the stuffy type.'

He was taken aback. More, the dark eyes were no longer expressionless. For a moment he was totally outraged.

'*Stuffy?*' The single word sounded very foreign all of a sudden.

Abby bit back a smile and rearranged her cutlery.

'I mean, you're not exactly *old,*' she said innocently.

He sat bolt upright. The waiter brought wine. He hardly even looked at the bottle, waving the man to pour.

'I am thirty-four,' he bit out.

'It must be all those millions,' said Abby with spurious sympathy.

He was deeply suspicious. 'What must?'

Abby was beginning to enjoy herself. She looked up and widened her eyes at him. 'Well, you're very serious, aren't you?'

But she had overplayed her hand. She saw him realise that she was winding him up. He relaxed and picked up his wine.

'Are you telling me to get a life, Lady Abigail?' he asked softly. And that caressing note was back with a vengeance.

Abby shivered like an animal, fascinated in spite of herself. 'I wouldn't dare,' she said, only half joking.

He lounged back in his chair and surveyed her. 'I've partied with experts, believe me.'

Abby looked at the strong handsome face—and the lithe body under his city suit. She remembered that body, glistening in the sun. She remembered him leaping like a dolphin to put all that glorious physical power behind his winning shot. She remembered the effect it had had on even sensible Señora Montijo.

Oh, yes, he would have partied with experts. Of course he had. A body like that wouldn't be allowed to do anything else. It stood to reason.

What was less reasonable was that it should make her own heart beat faster at the thought. Why did she suddenly feel as if she was the prey he was stalking through some dark forest? She wasn't afraid of party animals. She knew too many, including at least three of her brothers.

And then she thought—that's the first clue to who he is. Empty car, empty flat and not a single bit of personal information at the meeting and a novice's guide to business principles in the car. But he's just told me something about the man he really is. Something personal. Her heart beat harder still.

She said hastily, 'Nothing to do with me, anyway. I shouldn't have said that.'

'Why not? Because I'm an important client?' There was an edge to the warm voice.

Abby was honestly shocked. 'No! Because you rescued me from the rain and brought me to dinner.'

He looked at her oddly. 'I see,' he said after a moment. 'Well, I haven't rescued you from very much yet. You were going to tell me the problem.'

Abby wished he hadn't reminded her. She bit her lip.

'So you can apply your famous entrepreneurial skills to my homeless state?' she asked. But her smile wavered.

'Sure, if necessary. So tell me—who have you been living with up to now?'

She tried not to wince. Her eyes fell. 'I've had the basement in a family house.'

He digested this. 'And now the boyfriend's mother wants you out?'

'*No.*' Her eyes flew to his face in astonishment. 'Where did you get that idea?'

He shrugged. 'It seemed the likeliest. So who is throwing you out?'

Abby swallowed. 'My father's wife,' she said in a brittle voice. 'My father's new wife.'

There was a little silence.

She seized her glass of wine and drank a great gulp as if it was water. She did not look at him but she could feel those steady dark eyes, unwavering. She had no idea what he was thinking.

Eventually he said, 'I think you'd better tell me everything.'

And to her astonishment, she did.

Everything. Not just her father coming back from his holiday married to Justine, but the years before when Abby left college early to run the Yorkshire house after the housekeeper left at a moment's notice. The struggle to maintain the jewel of a house on a shoestring. The beauty of the countryside; the loneliness when her father was travelling, now that all her brothers moved on; her shyness.

When she had finished he said, 'Poor Cinderella.'

Abby was startled. 'I'm not a Cinderella. I'm an independent woman with a career of my own. I just started a bit late, that's all.'

'And now you don't have a roof over your head.'

She sighed. 'I'll have to go to a hotel, I suppose. Maybe if I go to one of the cheapo tourist places they won't recognise the name.'

He pulled a face. 'A student dive? The blankets will be

thin and too short and you'll spend the night listening to the television next door.'

Abby was amused in spite of herself. 'What do you know about student dives?'

'I haven't always been in the important-client class,' Emilio said dryly. 'You'd be amazed at some of the dumps I've stayed in.'

Another clue to the mystery that was Emilio Diz?

'It sounds like it,' said Abby, distracted.

'You deserve better than that.'

She was surprisingly touched. 'Thank you.'

'You could always go somewhere decent and I could pay the bill,' he suggested.

Abby shuddered at the thought. 'The point is to *avoid* scandal,' she said firmly. 'Anyway, I can't borrow money from strangers.'

'You wouldn't be borrowing money. I'd just be making a payment on your behalf,' he said fluently.

'And you think that wouldn't get into the papers?' mocked Abby. 'Your name would be even more of a news item than mine.'

He sighed. 'You're right, of course.'

'So back to Plan A.'

He frowned down at his plate. He had only been playing with his *penne alla Norma* ever since the waiter put the dish in front of him. Now he put his fork down.

'Not necessarily.' He leaned forward. 'Look, I've got a problem, too. Maybe we could help each other.'

'Oh? What sort of problem?'

Abby wasn't exactly suspicious but she wasn't going to commit herself to wholehearted support of any scheme thought up by Emilio Diz until he was a little more specific. She didn't trust him. Nobody made millions by the time they were thirty-four without being tricky, not if they'd started out in student dives.

He saw her reservations and laughed softly. 'I need a woman.'

Abby dropped her fork. She felt the colour flood into her cheeks like the stain would seep across this paper tablecloth if she tipped her excellent glass of wine onto it. Her eyes flew to his.

'Isn't that what you expected me to say?' he asked, smooth as honey.

'No, of course not,' she said with heat. 'It's not the sort of thing people *do* say. Not just come out with it like that across a dinner table.' She flapped her hands helplessly. 'Not in my experience.'

He smiled but the dark eyes were not amused. He would be an implacable enemy, Abby thought suddenly.

But all he said was, 'Then I've widened your experience. I told you I would.'

'Anyway, I don't believe it's true.' Too late, she recognised mockery. At once fury replaced her embarrassment. And, as always when she lost her temper, she lost her sense of self-preservation to go with it.

'Men as rich as you must have women falling over themselves to do whatever you want,' she said waspishly. 'Even if you have forgotten about cool cars.'

His eyes flared.

Got you, thought Abby with satisfaction. *You weren't expecting that.*

He smiled. Abby wondered whether tigers smiled when they sighted their prey through the undergrowth. She knew just how they would look.

'You think my wealth would make a woman overlook the fact that I'm a bore?' His tone was affable—and very, *very* Latin.

Maybe getting him on the raw hadn't been such a good idea after all. Now she came to think of it, he probably hadn't got that rich at thirty-four by letting people score points off him, either.

'Er—'

'And of course you are right.' Very Latin, very sober. He met her eyes candidly.

She didn't trust him an inch.

'O-oh?'

'To be very frank, women are a problem for me.'

Not an inch, not a centimetre, not a millimetre, thought Abby indignantly.

'Really?' she said with a snap.

'Of course I'm not alone in that.'

'Have you tried a lonely hearts column?'

He ignored that. 'There is a whole generation of us. The Cyber Millionaires, they call us. We do what we love—it makes us a fortune and then—wham!'

He clapped his hands together. To Abby's acute embarrassment, heads turned sharply. Emilio was magnificently unaware. He leaned forward.

'We can't afford to marry,' he told her, his eyes tragic. 'Our lives are ruined.'

'Oh, sure,' said Abby with irony. 'Why can't you afford to marry? Don't like narrowing your options down to one woman?'

The tragic look disappeared to be replaced by speculation. 'You don't believe me.'

'I believe you'll do whatever you want, whenever you want, whether you can afford to or not,' she said with asperity.

His eyes flickered. There was a sharp little silence.

Abby thought, startled, *I've got him again. And I wasn't even trying...*

He said eventually, 'You ought to meet my lawyer. That's exactly what he's afraid of. I get notes from him all the time.'

'Sorry?'

'We are talking about community property and the fact that prenuptial agreements aren't reliable,' he explained.

'I don't understand.'

'If the marriage falls apart, the lady could walk with half my stake in the company. Independent shareholders won't stand for it. So if I want to float the company, I have to stay celibate.'

It was too much, when he had been sitting there, purring and predatory as a tiger all through the meal.

'Celibate?' said Abby in disbelieving reflex.

He gave a slow smile.

Instantly she felt as if she had been boiled in oil.

Why did I say that? Why don't I think before I open my mouth?

Another hideous flush threatened. Abby fought it, struggling to find a neutral expression. She knew that he was watching in deep appreciation. She seethed—and dropped her fork into her pasta.

His smile grew. 'Well, single,' he allowed. His voice was slow, deep and dripping with sexual innuendo.

Abby swigged her wine as if it was water again. This time she choked.

'I can see you're just breaking your heart over it,' she said, when she could speak.

He laughed aloud at that. 'I'm not looking for a wife at the moment,' he admitted. 'But I do need some female help quite badly.'

'Oh, yes?' Abby said noncommittally.

'You've seen the apartment.' He spread his hands. 'I need someone to furnish it.'

She stared. 'So employ an interior decorator.'

'I did. That was him on the phone this evening. I fired him.'

'I heard. Maybe you ought to call him back and unfire him.'

'He won't do what I want. He's turning it into his great work of art. He wants me to wait ten weeks to get a decent bed. God knows how long it will take to have somewhere to sit down.' He looked at her pleadingly. 'What I need is a sensible woman who knows the London shops and will get me some furniture *fast*.'

Abby thought, I could do that. I could *really* do that. But—do I want to? Buying furniture for a man—for this man—seemed more personal than she wanted to get. Especially with a man who gave away so few clues about himself.

Except he's dropped his guard twice with me already.

Somehow that made it seem even more hazardous.

She said hurriedly, 'Why don't you ask the porters? They usually have connections everywhere.'

'Tried that. It's got me a borrowed bed until the end of the week.'

'That's all?'

He shrugged. 'The block is new. The porters are all new. I guess they haven't got their networks up and running yet.'

She felt as if she were drowning. 'You must have friends who would help. Family...'

'Sure. I tried calling my oldest sister. No answer. I even rang the office to track her down. They told me to get real. It's February. Everyone who doesn't have to be in BA is at the beach.'

'She'll be back, though.'

'Sure. Could be two weeks. Could be three. And then she'll take time to get over here. Meanwhile I'm sleeping on the floor from Saturday.'

Abby said desperately, 'I've never done anything like it.'

'But this flat of yours—you furnished that?'

'Well, yes,' she admitted reluctantly.

'Then you can help me. I'm not fussy. It doesn't have to last for ever. Just get the basics until I have time to think about it properly.'

She looked at him. He was not purring at her now. There was none of that deliberate charm. He just looked desperately tired, all of a sudden. Abby's tender heart, always her downfall, went out to him.

'All right.'

He gave her a blinding flash of white teeth. The look of tiredness disappeared as if it had never been.

'Great. It's a deal.' He held out a hand across the table.

Abby took it reluctantly. She had the uncomfortable feeling she had been duped.

He said cheerfully, 'You put my household together. You stay as long as you like. Excellent use of resources. You solve my problem, I solve yours.'

'I hope so,' said Abby.

She had a nasty feeling that a whole portfolio of new problems was just about to open up in front of her.

CHAPTER SIX

THE first problem that night was the bed. There was only one.

'You take it,' said Emilio.

Abby was conscience stricken. 'I couldn't. I wished myself on to you. I'll—'

'My dear girl, are you seriously suggesting that you sleep on the floor while I take the best sprung mattress the twenty-first century can offer?'

'Yes. Why not?'

He gave a sigh of pure exasperation. 'Get real.'

'Get real yourself,' said Abby with spirit. 'The only reason why you should sleep on the floor instead of me is some macho thing.'

Emilio stiffened. 'Excuse me?'

'Which is totally outdated.'

He was furious.

'When did courtesy go out of fashion?'

'But it's not courtesy. It's patronising. You wouldn't tell a man who landed himself on you like this to take the only bed. But I'm a woman—'

'At least we agree on something,' he murmured.

Abby ignored that. 'So you think you have to treat me as if I'm a fragile little flower.'

'Oh, is that what I'm doing?'

She ignored that, too. 'It's not necessary. And it's not respectful.'

'So I should let you sleep on the floor to show how much I respect you?'

'Yes,' said Abby confused.

'Then I'm sorry, I don't respect you enough.'

Their eyes locked. Abby was quite simply glaring but Emilio's expression was a lot more complicated. The dark brown eyes were intent as if he was trying to make out the intricacy of some intriguing object. Meeting that intensity head-on, Abby felt her heart jolt. For a tiny moment, it felt as if the thick new carpet and even the floor had dissolved under her. She was hurtling through space while those dark eyes watched, interested...

Reason, she thought hurriedly. That's what men respond to.

Abby had dealt with her four brothers since she was a baby. Since she was twelve she had run their household. She knew there was no point in yelling at men, no matter how right you were. In fact the more right you were, the less point there was in yelling. You just had to present them with reasoned arguments. That way, sometimes, they could be brought to admit you had a case.

All she had to do was tell herself that the floor was solid, wrench her attention back from those mesmeric eyes, and *concentrate*. So...

She made her tone as conciliatory as she knew how. 'It won't hurt me. I have slept on the floor lots of times.'

'Not,' said Emilio grimly, 'with me.'

Every single argument went out of her head. She just stood there, gawping at him, wordless. The phrase rang round her head like a church bell, drowning everything else.

With me. *With me.*

He looked amused.

Of course, he had not actually said, *you sleep with me.* Had probably not even thought it. Only now, with her opening and closing her mouth like a stranded fish, he was going to think of it all right. She could not have reacted more strongly if he had suggested a full seduction, thought Abby in despair. The idea was there with them now, flying around in the empty room like an escapee from Pandora's box.

Suddenly every half-remembered erotic fantasy she had

ever had returned to join in the fun. She was no longer arguing with an impatient man in an unfurnished flat. There was music. Unseen candlelight.

The man in question took on a new aspect. He was no longer either a difficult client or a bad memory. He had all the mystery of a masked stranger in the shadows. But a stranger she half expected and a mask she wanted to penetrate.

Oh, Lord, thought Abby, startled.

Her clothing seemed to loosen somehow. Under it, her body realised it was beautiful. She stood taller. The air was suddenly full of the scent of roses.

Her skin shivered as if he had touched her. Abby found she was holding her breath.

But she did not need to.

'Sorry,' said Emilio, laughing. 'That could have been better phrased.'

Abby swallowed and started breathing again. She felt as if her cheeks were on fire.

'Yes, it could,' she said curtly.

He looked at her curiously. 'Are you all right?'

'I'm fine.'

'Are you sure?'

She shook her head irritably at the fantasies. They mocked her. But they wouldn't go *away*.

'I just don't think it was very funny.'

'So teasing is out? As well as chivalry?'

'Chivalry is a patriarchal concept,' snapped Abby, goaded.

She did not believe it but, with all those images of clothes falling off still waving about in her imagination, she had to do something. Going to war was as good a strategy as any. And this was stuff she knew. She had heard Molly di Perretti say it often enough.

'What the hell are you talking about?'

'The whole point of chivalry is to keep women helpless,'

announced Abby. She was on a roll now. 'And we're supposed to be grateful for it.'

Emilio was outraged. 'If this is gratitude, I think I'll pass.'

Of course, that reminded her that she did, indeed, owe him a debt of gratitude. He had rescued her from something close to despair tonight, to say nothing of the weather. He had fed her and listened to her and then he had come up with a solution to her problem. What was more, there was no one else she could turn to tonight. He was putting a roof over her head and here she was, screaming at him.

Her eyes fell.

'Sorry,' she muttered.

Emilio was silent for a moment. Then he said in an odd voice, 'You're in a real mess, aren't you?'

Abby looked up, shocked. Surely he couldn't have picked up her brief romantic fantasy, back there?

'What do you mean?' Her voice jumped all over the place.

Emilio was already turning away. 'We're due a long talk about men and women and a sense of proportion. But not tonight. You're wiped.'

A sense of proportion? Oh, heavens, he *had* picked up that surge of longing. She set her teeth.

'I don't need you to analyse me,' she said rudely to hide her wincing.

'You don't know what you need,' said Emilio quite kindly.

Abby lifted her chin. 'So what do you suggest?' She flung it at him like a challenge.

'A bath. Then a good night's sleep in that bed,' he said literally. 'Things are always more manageable in the morning.'

Abby's chin went up even higher. He sounded so damned superior, she thought mutinously. But she knew he was right. Perversely that annoyed her even more.

Even though a warm bath sounded like heaven, she was not going to do anything he said without a fight.

'You've got guest towels then, have you? Even though you haven't got any furniture?' she taunted.

For a moment the black brows twitched together in annoyance. So there were some things he did not have an answer for, thought Abby in unworthy triumph.

Then he said equally, 'I haven't the slightest idea. Let's look.'

The guest bathroom was bare but there was a collection of towels of assorted sizes, still in their packets in the master bathroom. Emilio stood in the doorway from the bedroom and looked at her. His smile that only just stopped short of triumph.

'Help yourself.'

Suddenly Abby was too tired to fight him anymore. She felt her shoulders sag and had to fight not to sink onto the bed behind her. She turned away to hide the fact that her eyes were filling with stupid tears. Simple tiredness, of course.

'You're very kind,' she said in a stifled voice.

She seemed to have been wearing the severe business jacket half her life. She shrugged out of it and let it fall with relief. It missed the bed and flopped onto the carpet. She thought she heard a stifled sound from Emilio but when she looked round at him he had crossed to the window and was staring out into the lamplit gardens below.

'I'll call the Hyde. See if they can let me have a room for one more night,' he mused.

Now that Abby had admitted to herself how tired she was, she did not have the energy for more than a token protest.

He looked at her, all the way across the bed. She could not read his expression but his eyes were searching.

'Will you be worried here on your own?'

She was surprised. 'No. Why should I?'

He seemed to choose his words carefully. 'Some people can't sleep in strange apartments.'

Abby flexed her stiff shoulders. 'I could sleep standing up in a ditch tonight,' she said ruefully.

He did not answer.

Just for a moment, she thought she could read his expression after all. He was staring at the place in the base of her throat where the pulse beat. And the expression was hunger.

But then his eyes flickered and he was giving her a cool smile. Abby decided that she must have been mistaken. After all, she had not seen a lot of hunger in men's eyes, she thought ruefully.

'Then sleep well.' He went to the door of the master suite, then paused. 'I'll be back tomorrow for breakfast. We need to get some things clear. Don't go to work before we've talked.'

Abby was too tired to object. She suppressed a yawn with difficulty.

'Whatever you say.'

He left.

Abby eased her stiff shoulders under the steaming water but she did not stay in the bath long. She knew there was a real risk of falling asleep. As it was, she seemed to be dreaming. Wildly improbable dreams, too, involving Emilio Diz and a rescue from pirates.

It was an old friend, that dream. Though it had not visited her since she was—well, how old? Sixteen was it?

Trying to decide, Abby found that she was slipping dangerously close to sleep and the water line. She shook herself awake and climbed out of the bath.

That wasn't going to start all over again, she told herself muzzily. It had been bad enough having an adolescent crush when she was sixteen. She had dragged herself through it then and she had got over it. But she wasn't going to go round for a second shot.

Emilio Diz had not seen her as a woman then. He was not seeing her as a woman now. Then, she had just been a starstruck teenager to him. Now she was a salvage project.

Neither, thought Abby, weaving her way to the bed wrapped in the biggest fluffiest bath towel she had ever seen, was attractive. So the sooner she stopped dreaming about him the better.

The exclusive hotel was much too gentlemanly to express surprise at Emilio's request. He had stayed there every time he came to London for several years. So had his family, of whom there were a number. He was a valued customer.

So yes, they were happy to accommodate Señor Diz for a further night. No, his lack of baggage was not a problem. They were discreetly incurious about the reasons for the change of plan. When he announced that his apartment was still not ready, they were even more discreetly sympathetic. And when he asked for an early morning call accompanied by a breakfast hamper for two from the kitchen, they became discretion personified.

'On the hunt?' the night porter asked the knowledgeable night desk manager after Emilio had run up the staircase to his first-floor suite.

'Of course,' said the manager. 'Though it's not like him.'

'What isn't?'

'They usually give him breakfast, not the other way round.'

'Maybe she's thrown him out,' suggested the porter.

'Women don't throw Emilio Diz out.'

'Maybe this time he's in love,' said the porter, a romantic.

'More likely, this time he's met his match,' said the manager, a realist.

He would have been surprised at how close he was to Emilio's own feelings on the matter.

He prowled the overheated hotel room restlessly. The woman was infuriating. Why on earth didn't she stand up for herself, instead of letting her father's new wife walk all over her like that? He had no patience with such spinelessness.

Except that she wasn't spineless. She had stood up to him

easily enough. More than stood up to him. Provoked him. Deliberately.

He nearly bumped into an antique coffee table at the thought.

Well, no, he corrected himself, sinking onto rather pretty Chippendale sofa and rubbing his shin absently. Not all the provocation was deliberate. Some of it—the worst of it—she was clearly completely unaware of.

He frowned. No women of her age *ought* to be unaware of provocation like that. He remembered the careless way she had let the jacket drop, as if she had completely forgotten what she was wearing underneath. And what she was *not* wearing.

Emilio closed his eyes. He could still feel that jolt of shock as she half turned, revealing the smooth naked skin of her back under all that criss-cross lacing. She had a small mole between her shoulder blades. He broke out in a sweat remembering.

For a crazy moment he had nearly cancelled the distance between them and bent his lips to that mole. It would have been so *easy*. It was what that apology of a top must have been designed for. She had no business wearing it if she didn't want a man to...

He curbed the direction of his thoughts.

Careful, he told himself. She was not inviting anything and you know it. The woman was asleep on her feet. She probably *had* forgotten what she was wearing underneath. She'd worn it to that damned meeting. She certainly wasn't inviting any advances there.

And she didn't invite any all evening. It would have been easy enough to give him the signal that she was available, after all. And she would know how to do it. She was not his little crane fly anymore. She was Lady Abigail Templeton Burke, with her turquoise hair and her drawling social confidence. She might not be able to deal with her stepmother but he would have put money on her having all the men she wanted on a string.

So if she did not give him a signal, it was because she did not want to.

Emilio frowned. Why didn't she want to? How could this awareness be one-sided?

But he knew the answer to that, too. That evening at the Montijo's place had been a turning point for him. Maybe that was why he had never forgotten his little crane fly. But she had been only just coming out of adolescence. There would have been lots of encounters like that for her. It was part of the growing up process. It would have been no big deal for her.

She probably doesn't even remember you, he told himself bracingly.

It was extraordinary how desolate that made him feel.

Abby woke with a jump. For a moment she did not know where she was. She stared at the bay window. It was in quite the wrong place and much too big. Come to that, the bed was even bigger and not one she recognised. The duvet cover was too crisp, it smelled wrong. And the pillows were all over the place. She closed her eyes and—

Not with me, said a voice in her head.

Abby's eyes flew open. She shot up in the borrowed bed as if an alarm had gone off. Emilio Diz! She was in his home, in his bed, heaven help her. After all these years of suppressing that particular memory, here she was full circle, facing her nemesis again.

Well, no. Not actually facing him. She was alone, in spite of the voice in her head. Wasn't she?

Abby looked round warily. But though the unfamiliar window was in his bedroom and there were two substantial matching suitcases standing in the corner, there was no sign of the man himself. He had haunted her dreams but he had had the decency to keep out of her room. No tell-tale inden-

The Harlequin Reader Service® — Here's how it works:

Accepting your 2 free books and gift places you under no obligation to buy anything. You may keep the books and gift and return the shipping statement marked "cancel." If you do not cancel, about a month later we'll send you 6 additional novels and bill you just $3.15 each in the U.S., or $3.59 each in Canada, plus 25¢ shipping & handling per book and applicable taxes if any.* That's the complete price and — compared to cover prices of $3.99 each in the U.S. and $4.50 each in Canada — it's quite a bargain! You may cancel at any time, but if you choose to continue, every month we'll send you 6 more books, which you may either purchase at the discount price or return to us and cancel your subscription.

*Terms and prices subject to change without notice. Sales tax applicable in N.Y. Canadian residents will be charged applicable provincial taxes and GST.

If offer card is missing write to: Harlequin Reader Service, 3010 Walden Ave., P.O. Box 1867, Buffalo NY 14240-1867

NO POSTAGE
NECESSARY
IF MAILED
IN THE
UNITED STATES

BUSINESS REPLY MAIL
FIRST-CLASS MAIL   PERMIT NO. 717-003   BUFFALO, NY

POSTAGE WILL BE PAID BY ADDRESSEE

HARLEQUIN READER SERVICE
3010 WALDEN AVE
PO BOX 1867
BUFFALO NY 14240-9952

GET FREE BOOKS and a FREE GIFT
WHEN YOU PLAY THE...

Just scratch off the silver box with a coin. Then check below to see the gifts you get!

SLOT MACHINE GAME!

YES! I have scratched off the silver box. Please send me the 2 free Harlequin Romance® books and gift for which I qualify. I understand I am under no obligation to purchase any books, as explained on the back of this card.

186 HDL DFS7
(H-R-OS-11/01)

386 HDL DFS9

NAME   (PLEASE PRINT CLEARLY)

ADDRESS

APT.#   CITY

STATE/PROV.   ZIP/POSTAL CODE

7 7 7 Worth TWO FREE BOOKS **plus a** BONUS **Mystery Gift!**

🍒🍒🍒 Worth TWO FREE BOOKS!

♣♣♣ Worth ONE FREE BOOK!

🔔🔔🍒 **TRY AGAIN!**

Visit us online at www.eHarlequin.com

DETACH AND MAIL CARD TODAY!

tation in the maltreated pillow beside her. No man's clothes strewn amongst her own.

She relaxed and looked at her watch. He said he would come to breakfast. Well, it was still early but she did not want to risk him finding her in bed. She got up.

Be honest, her sensible side urged her. You're not a bit worried about what he would do if he found you in bed. You're worried about what *you* would do. You've only got to look at him and you remember the way he made you feel, even though he didn't know it. Even though he turned you down, just like any grown man ought to turn down a teenage groupie.

But I've grown out of my teenage groupie stage.

Yes, but he's still heartthrob material.

'Still gorgeous after all these years,' said Abby aloud. 'Just my luck.'

Yup, agreed her more sensible self, not very encouragingly. You only have to look at the man to go weak at the knees. You're going to have to watch that.

She turned the shower down to cool and stepped grimly under it.

Which was why she did not hear Emilio's key, or the door open, or him call her name.

She did smell coffee but she thought it was another illusion. It reminded her though that she could do with a cup if there were any stores in Emilio's inter-galactic kitchen. Wrapped in a bath towel, with her turquoise hair under a towel, she padded out to have look.

'Good morning,' said Emilio, from behind his *Financial Times.* He was propped up at the breakfast bar, looking totally at home. And as if he had been there for hours.

Abby's hands flew to the towelling knot between her breasts. The bath towel was thick and fluffy and covered her from the armpit to well below the knee. But she suddenly felt naked.

'You're early.' It sounded like an accusation.

'Indeed I am.'

He lowered the pink pages and gave her a neutral smile. It fizzed along her nerve endings as if he had touched her. On the marble tiled floor her toes curled in pure reflex.

Make that impure reflex, thought Abby, hot. Her hold tightened on the knot in her bath towel.

'I wasn't expecting you till later. I'll get dressed.'

'Take your time. I have work I can catch up on.'

Abby took in the hotel's elegant green canvas cool bag on the work top, the cup of coffee in front of Emilio.

'You came prepared, I see.'

'I'm always prepared. I was going to give you until eight, then do the Sleeping Beauty routine,' he told her blandly.

Their eyes met.

Abby had a vision—as detailed as those disturbing dreams—of Emilio coming into that huge bedroom, bending over the huge bed, kissing her awake as she lay among the tumbled pillows...

She gulped. Glared. And fled.

Left alone, Emilio smiled for the first time since he had left the flat last night. Well, at least the awareness wasn't one-sided this morning, he thought. That was a step in the right direction.

He did not stop to examine which direction that was.

Abby had a horrible struggle with her fashionable gear. Yesterday she had had help to put on Ravi's new creation. Now she found exactly how difficult it was to lace up the dashing little top.

At last, she gave in and admitted defeat. It was not what she wanted. She would have given anything in the world not to have to ask Emilio for help. But there was nothing for it.

Holding the scrap of silk to her breasts like a Celtic shield, she padded back to the kitchen.

'I've got a bit of a problem,' she said, too loudly, too aggressively.

In the middle of sipping his coffee, Emilio looked up. His eyes widened.

'I've tried and tried and it's just getting worse,' said Abby hurriedly. 'It's like trying to lace your trainers in the mirror and behind your back all at the same time. My dexterity is not up to it.'

'I'm not surprised,' said Emilio, after an infinitesimal pause. 'Let me have a look.'

Abby went close and presented her back to him. She felt his fingers, light as moth wings, at her spine, her waist, her shoulder blade.

She talked all the time, to take her mind off that disturbing friction.

'Why do they make things like this? I don't see the point. You need a lady's maid to put it on. I didn't realise when I bought it because Ravi put it on and any fool can get it off.'

'I think you may just have answered your own question,' said Emilio dryly, his fingers busy.

Abby prudently decided not to pursue that one. She twisted round, trying to look over her shoulder. 'Is it hopeless?'

'You've got it in a bit of a tangle,' he told her. 'Not beyond my skill. Just stand still.'

But that was more difficult than Abby would have believed possible.

'There's no way to do it,' she said. 'I tried and tried. If you lace it tight, you can't get it over your shoulders. If you lace it loose, it gets all tied up round itself. Either way, there's no way to pull the laces tight after you've got it on.'

She sounded like an idiot, chattering feverishly. But anything was better than listening to his steady breathing, feeling his breath in her hair as he concentrated on the cat's cradle she was wearing. The trouble was, she wanted him to concentrate on her, not her brain teaser garments. And she didn't want his breathing to be steady, either.

He said, 'Who's Ravi?'

'What?' Abby was piqued. She didn't want him making

idle conversation, either. 'Oh, he's the designer. I shall tell him, he needs to forget silk drawstring. He's got to think about stretch fabrics if he's going to lace things up like—'

And then Emilio's fingers brushed her nape and she stopped dead. She felt as if she had walked into a wall of ice. Then fire. Then ice again.

'There,' said Emilio in a satisfied voice.

He stepped back.

'Thank you,' said Abby. It sounded strangled.

He went to the Hyde's picnic bag and started to unpack it. He gave her one of his unreadable smiles. To Abby, still quivering, it felt as if someone had opened the door of a furnace.

She flinched, and half turned away. It was as if some instinct was telling her to protect herself from the blast, she thought. She leaned against the breakfast bar rather suddenly.

'I'm sorry we have to eat on the hoof,' said Emilio, apparently sublimely unaware. 'See if you can get a table and chairs to go in here by this evening. They don't have to be beautiful. We can always get rid of them later. Just somewhere to sit and eat in comfort.'

He gave her a neat dish of melon and papaya and a small silver spoon.

'Right,' said Abby, tasting the fruit. The spoon had a crest on it. She inspected it idly. It was the hotel's. Clearly the picnic had come complete with all accessories. She thought suddenly: you have to be seriously rich to get a hotel to organise something like this at a moment's notice.

Remembering how rich he was, somehow underlined the difference between them. It was like a shower of cold water. But after the first shock, it helped. Normality was a close shore. She could get back there.

She pulled herself together with an effort. 'And you'll need some basic cutlery, as well.'

He nodded. 'Do you want to make a list?'

'I'd better,' she agreed.

The deep internal quivering was calming down. Thank God for practical problems, thought Abby.

He gave her coffee. Then turned to his briefcase and pulled out a slim folder.

'I've been through this once with the interior designer. This is the brief I gave him. Have a look at it and see what you think you can manage.'

Abby cast an eye down the closely typed sheets. When she looked up, all trace of quivering was gone. She was sensible, practical Abby again.

'You know, I think it would be a mistake to rush into buying all this. You can hire furniture. I'd suggest you do that for a few weeks while you think about how you want the place to look.'

He shrugged, massively uninterested. 'Whatever. Can you do that for me?'

'Yes,' she said with total conviction.

Because she could. Practical things she could handle. She had always been practical. It was only wicked stepmothers and men who wanted her to play Sleeping Beauty that gave her problems.

'Fine. Go ahead. Get whatever you think best. Now, money—' He extracted a sliver of plastic from his wallet and handed it across to her. It was followed by a business card. 'Use that. If you have any difficulty get them to call me. I'll get an account set up for you to draw on but it will take a couple of days.

'Keys.' He gave her a set on a beautiful silver key ring. 'There's no burglar alarm so you don't have to worry about sprinting to beat the beep.'

Abby took the keys. 'OK. Look, I've got stuff to do today. I can't just take time off at a moment's notice. I'm not sure how much I can get organised by tonight.'

'Sure. Just do what you can.'

Emilio was already closing his briefcase. That's me dealt

with, thought Abby. On to the next thing now Abby's got her tasks for the day! It was a feeling she was familiar with.

She said quietly, 'I live to serve.' The mockery had an edge.

He was shrugging himself into his well-cut jacket but he paused at that. His eyes raked her, frowning.

'Not me,' he said abruptly. He took hold of her chin, forcing her to meet his eyes. 'We cooperate,' he said softly. 'You don't serve me. As long as it suits us both, we cooperate. The moment one of us feel exploited, it's over. Clear?'

'Clear,' said Abby, oddly shaken.

He let go her chin.

'Good.' The change in his mood was like lightning. 'Then I'll see you tonight.'

'That sounds so domestic,' she said involuntarily.

'So it does.' The dark eyes were dancing suddenly. 'Have a good day. Dear.'

Before she knew what he was doing, he bent and kissed her lips. It was light, familiar, mischievous. And *heart-stopping*.

Abby made a small, shocked sound and leaned heavily on the breakfast bar to keep her legs from folding under her.

Emilio looked quite simply delighted.

'This,' he said, 'was meant to be. Genius. Pure genius.'

And went.

CHAPTER SEVEN

To HER own astonishment, Abby got to work early. Dazed but early.

'Hi,' said Molly, a morning person, looking up from her computer screen.

'Hard night?'

'What?'

'You look a bit ragged.'

'D-do I?'

'Not only ragged but wearing yesterday's gear. Very suspicious. Who's the lucky man?'

Abby managed not to blush by dint of looking Molly straight in the eye.

'Do you think I'm really the sort of girl who spends the night with a guy she picks up?'

'Hey, who said he had to be a pick-up? For all I know, you were out on the town with the love of your life.'

This time Abby did not manage to fight down the betraying colour. 'Oh, yes?'

'And then it just all got too much for you,' said Molly dreamily. 'Carried away by passion.'

Abby took refuge in heavy sarcasm. 'Oh, yes, that sounds like me, doesn't it? Passion! Huh! Got a name for this mythical love of my life?'

Molly flung up her hands in a gesture of surrender.

'I'm just pointing out that you're still wearing your fashion show outfit,' she said, amused. 'I'm not the morality police. Who, where and why you did it, is your business.'

'I didn't—' began Abby furiously. She broke off. 'You're winding me up again, right?'

'You're learning,' said Molly with regret. She pushed her

chair back and tipped her booted heels onto the desk. 'I hear you had a really good row with the new client yesterday. Give you a sleepless night?'

Abby was annoyed. 'That didn't take you long. Did they call you at home to tell you about it?'

'The e-mail is humming,' said Molly unrepentant. She waved a hand at the screen. 'First thing I saw when I opened it this morning. Two first-hand reports and God knows how many have-you-heards.'

It startled Abby.

'It wasn't *that* big a row.'

Molly laughed. 'Any row is big for you, babe. I've never met a woman with less temperament in my life.'

'Don't you believe it,' said Abby with feeling.

'No, it's true. This place lurches from crisis to crisis. You just take it all in your stride. Nothing gets to you.'

She should have seen her this morning, Abby thought. That kiss had got to her, all right. It could not have been more casual. But it had rocked her to her toes.

Molly was more perceptive than she liked to pretend. She saw Abby's reaction.

'What's wrong?' she said, abandoning the teasing manner.

Abby hesitated. For a moment the urge to confide was almost overwhelming.

But then Molly said, 'I see you're in the papers again this morning,' and Abby thought better of it.

Until she told her family, it was better that nobody knew that Justine had thrown her out of the house. And as for Emilio—well, what was there to confide? He had given her a roof over her head and offered her a deal that would keep it there until she could get herself sorted out. The man was a knight in shining armour but that was where the romance ended. He saw her as a charity case, who needed rescuing. Anything else was all in her imagination.

So she pulled herself together and said, 'What are the papers saying this time?'

Molly waved at the screen. Abby peered over her shoulder.

C&C put together a daily digest of all the media attention any of their clients received. Abby wasn't a client but C&C had just started tracking all mentions of the agency or its personnel, as well. One person came in early every morning to go through the papers and the monitoring services' lists of the previous day's radio and television broadcasts. By the time most people arrived for work, the list was up on the office mail.

This week it was Molly's turn.

She said now, 'You get three mentions. The usual suspects,' she added, referring to the popular tabloids.

'Oh, dear.'

'Don't worry. You were clearly in a supporting role. Diane Ladrot gets the headlines.'

Abby gave a sigh of undisguised relief. 'That's all right then.'

'Mind you,' said Molly naughtily, 'I'm not sure they'd seen the hair before they submitted their copy. What happened to it?'

Abby went to her own desk and started to organise herself. 'Diane Ladrot had a spare hairdresser lying about.'

'Cool.'

Abby switched on her computer. She did not look at Molly.

'What do you think?'

Molly did not hesitate. 'It's certainly interesting.'

'You hate it.'

'No, I don't. I don't. I think it's great. Just a bit of a departure.' She looked at her friend curiously. 'Are you going to turn into a raver, Abby?'

Abby switched on her computer and banged the keyboard with unnecessary vigour.

'Not very likely, is it?'

Molly considered that seriously. 'Oh, I don't know.

You've been a good girl a long time. Could be time for a change.'

Abby was so startled, she stopped attacking the keyboard. 'What?'

'Well, you've got the figure. Your title has got you the press coverage,' she said practically. 'And now you've got the hair,' she added with a little choke of laughter. 'All you need is a glamorous man.'

There was a nasty silence.

Then, 'Oh, is that all?' said Abby in a hollow voice.

Absorbed in her theoretical press campaign for Abby's supposed new persona, Molly didn't notice.

'A good public row wouldn't do any harm, either.'

'Oh.'

'Maybe you should get in touch with that little twerp, Deor Spiro, again. Throw a glass of wine over him at a nightclub and you're home free. The capital's newest It girl.'

'I can't wait.'

Molly laughed. 'Don't sound so depressed. It's all publicity. That's what everyone here is aiming for.'

'I thought we were aiming for *good* publicity.'

Molly widened her eyes, all innocence. 'Nothing wrong with being an It girl. Very glamorous.'

Abby was dry. 'Good publicity never misrepresents the underlying product,' she quoted.

'You could be glamorous if you wanted to. Glamour is all in the mind.'

'Quite.'

'Well, if you didn't want to be glamorous, you should have passed on the peacock's tail hair,' said Molly without sympathy. 'That's going to put you well and truly in the spotlight. What have you got on today?'

'No functions. I'm in the office all day, thank God.' Abby looked at her client list. 'One children's book, one bottled water company, one organic campaigner. All regional or local.'

Molly chuckled. 'Look out Radio Scunthorpe. The Fab Ab is coming your way.'

Abby picked up a fistful of paper clips and threw them at her.

Emilio was setting up an office in Traynor's, to the unexpressed dismay of the management team.

'I'll make my headquarters here until I get myself sorted out in London,' Emilio told them blandly. 'I can keep an eye on developments. You can consult me when you need. Two birds with one stone.'

'Convenient,' said the managing director. He succeeded in not gnashing his teeth but it was a struggle.

Emilio bit back a smile. 'And I'd like to borrow a PA.'

But after that he relented. He refused to evict any of the directors from their offices. He camped out in a small meeting room, in which he installed the young trainee he had selected to act as PA because he spoke some Spanish.

'My address book,' he said, giving Gary a diskette. 'My schedule is on there, too. Will you call my office in Madrid and BA to make sure that they're all working from the same diary? And check that there aren't any urgent messages while you're about it.'

There was one, of course. In Emilio's experience there usually was when he was out of touch with his family for more than a week. This time it was Isabel from the beach house, worrying about the garbage not being collected back in BA, and Federico in Zurich with a crisis of confidence over his career.

Emilio frowned over the message. Federico was easily dealt with. Federico just needed to talk, to use his elder brother as a sounding board. Federico was on top of life, these days. A telephone call would probably do it.

But Isabel was different. Emilio doubted very much if the problem had anything to do with garbage. But, if she was trying to track him down across Europe, he was perfectly certain that the problem was real.

As real as his own problem, now that he had time to stand back from it.

Should he tell Abby that they had met before? She didn't remember. That much was obvious. Or at least, if she remembered the incident, she didn't associate him with the man she had kissed under the stars in the Montijo's garden.

Have I changed so much? thought Emilio, torn between annoyance and an odd relief.

She had been so young. So honest. That innocent kiss, in all its unpractised fervour, had stayed with him long after he forgot more skilful embraces. It was not a child's kiss. There was passion in it, a half knowledge of her own power—and his. But it was completely spontaneous. It felt like a first kiss, for both of them in a way. Surely that was not forgettable?

Maybe she had not forgotten, after all. Any more than he had. But what would she say if he suddenly announced, 'I'm not the boring businessman you think I am, I'm the guy who kissed you in the garden all those years ago'?

But there was a core of cool logic in Emilio that had guided him through his business career. It took over now.

She had known his name, his little crane fly. She had said, 'You're Emilio Diz. You're *famous*.' If she wanted to, she could remember that he was the man who had shared that moment out of time with her. If she did not remember it was because she did not want to.

The thing to do, he told himself, is find out *why* she doesn't want to.

He brought himself back to the present problem with an effort.

'Tell the BA office, I'll call my sister at the beach house this evening,' he said. 'Ask them to pass it on.'

He put his personal affairs to one side.

'Now, I want a talk to every member of management, starting with,' he consulted his personnel chart and chose a name from the middle rank, 'the manager of project evaluations. The sooner I get started on the detail, the sooner I can think about strategy. First things first.'

Abby went through her list of calls faster than she expected. That left her time to telephone a stylist that C&C sometimes recommended to their clients. Five minutes later she had the telephone numbers of four separate firms which rented furniture. One was even close enough to visit in her lunch hour.

'Sam, how are we off for cover?'

It was an unwritten rule that the office was never left unattended. Voice mail was never enough. Clients expected to talk to a real person if they called the main switchboard. So someone was always on duty.

Sam looked at the roster on the wall behind her desk. 'Looks OK if you want to take a long lunch today.'

Abby looked dubious.

'Or do you want some time off?'

'Probably. I'll have some furniture being delivered. I'm just not sure how soon they can do it. But maybe the porters can see it in if I ask them nicely.'

Sam's eyebrows rose. 'Refurbishing?'

'In a way,' said Abby uncomfortably. 'Anyway, how's it looking?'

'This week we're pretty full in the office. Next week is not so good. Can you get the stuff in before Friday?'

'If I can manage it, I'll get it in before tonight,' said Abby with feeling.

Her conscience still smote her about Emilio's unscheduled night in the hotel.

Sam was amused. 'You don't hang about when you make your mind up, do you? Well, no problem from the cover point of view. As long as you've done your own clients' work, you can take as much time as you want. In fact, if you want to take the rest of the day sticking twigs into your nest, you go out and get on with it.'

'Thank you,' said Abby with real gratitude.

She took Emilio's list and went.

The manager of the furniture warehouse went out of his way to be helpful. At first Abby was overwhelmed by the enthusiasm with which he whipped her round their riverside warehouse. She could not understand it. She was not one of their high-spending film set decorators and she was not going to rent much or for long. Surely she did not merit this much attention.

But then she reflected. C&C was a good customer and an even better source of referrals. So it was not surprising that they were so accommodating. And the manager was nice.

She had done the deal inside an hour. They made no fuss at all about using Emilio's credit card. They dismissed with scorn Abby's suggestion that they check her bona fides. They would not dream of checking with Señor Diz that she was authorised to use it. The name of C&C was reference enough.

They could even deliver by the end of the day, the manager assured her His assistant opened his mouth, encountered a bland smile from his boss, and shut it again.

'Since it is going to an address in central London, it will be easy. We can have this lot loaded and run it along south of the river. Best wait till after the rush hour, though. Shall we say seven-thirty?'

'Thank you,' said Abby.

She was surprised but relieved. It gave her time to pick up some cutlery and simple crockery before she had to be back to receive the furniture. She could also take the opportunity to go back to the garden flat while Justine was almost certainly out of the house on one of her shopping expeditions.

She really needed to pick up some of her things, thought Abby. The sooner she got out of Ravi's shoestring-backed sex trap the better. Nobody but Molly had mentioned it but eyes at C&C were sharp.

So she said seven-thirty would be fine, signed the invoice and left at a brisk pace.

'She's in a hurry,' said the manager, looking after her with a smile.

'So are we,' said the assistant in some dudgeon. 'How on earth are we going to get that stuff loaded and delivered today? We'll have to postpone all the other jobs.'

'So postpone them,' said the manager, unmoved.

'And delivering that late! We'll have to pay the guys overtime.'

'Cheap at the price.'

'But why?' cried the assistant. 'C&C aren't that good customers.'

'Do you know who that is?'

'Some gopher from—'

'No, she's not a gopher. That, my boy, is Lady Abigail Templeton Burke. She's just ditched some pop star, according to the papers. And here she is ordering up a new home's worth of furniture for a guy they used to call the Romeo of the tennis courts.'

'So?'

'So doesn't it sound to you as if they're moving in together?'

The assistant shrugged, unimpressed. 'Furniture rented by the month? Doesn't sound like they expect it to last,' he pointed out.

The manager closed his eyes in exquisite appreciation of his coup.

'Doesn't, does it?' he said with satisfaction. 'That, my boy, is why we're delivering this one as a priority. And the later we get there, the greater the chance that Romeo will be home. The papers will pay good money for photographs of those two.'

The house looked dark in the gloomy February afternoon. Dark and unfriendly. Abby folded her lips together.

She could remember, all too vividly, tumbling out of the car outside the front steps, glad to be released after the long journey from Yorkshire. Her mother had been ill then, and tired, but she could still laugh at Abby's eagerness. Abby remembered the way her father had scooped her mother out of the car and carried her up the steps. Abby, swelling with importance, had been allowed to unlock the front door.

Standing in the cold, empty street, fifteen years later, she could see it as clearly as if the little family were still there in the welcoming open door. Her father had switched on the light. The house had been so warm.

Little Abby had looked up and seen the way her mother rubbed her cheek against her father's collar; the way he dropped a kiss on her hair as he manoeuvred her into the hallway. It was so quick. So instinctive. So utterly ordinary. As if they loved each other so much that they touched all the time, the way they breathed, without noticing.

Abby felt her eyes sting. She blew her nose.

This is silly, she told herself. Your father was not going to stay in mourning for the rest of his life. Of course he wasn't. You shouldn't want him to.

But, oh, why did it have to be someone like Justine?

Abby swallowed. Well, it was Justine and there was nothing she could do about it.

Maybe Justine had qualities that Abby hadn't managed to find. Maybe she was insecure and just needed to have her new husband to herself when he came back from his business trip. Well, it was a chance. So the only thing for Abby to do was get out and leave them to it.

And forget that this house had ever been a family home.

Abby ran down the basement steps and let herself into her flat, trying hard not to think that it might be for the last time.

She packed fast and efficiently. She did not have many clothes. They all went into a suitcase. She stuffed her shoes into a squashy exercise roll along with her sponge bag. Then she stood back, looking round.

Everything here had been familiar since she was child. The china King Charles spaniels, one with a chipped ear. The grandfather clock with its baritone tick. The portrait of her great-great-grandmother in its faded oval mount. The candlesticks. The children's books…

Abby looked at the bags by the door. They were not that heavy.

She could not manage the grandfather clock. And the candlesticks were too valuable. But there was room for a few books surely?

Crazy. Pure sentimentality. Abby knew it. How on earth could she even think of taking those battered objects into Emilio's pristine apartment?

'But I want to read them to my own children,' she whispered.

Emilio would just have to get used to it.

It was a revelation.

Emilio paused outside the door of his new apartment. He was conscious of an odd sensation. He had moved into countless apartments since he reached adulthood in ten cities or more. This one was neither the grandest nor the most attractive. Yet he had never before felt like this when he stood at his front door with his key in his hand.

It wasn't—ridiculous idea—pride of ownership. Was it?

He had been proud of his first flat. He remembered that. He had been even more proud when he bought the big house in BA and collected his scattered family again. He had felt triumphant. He had beaten fate and the system then.

He was not feeling triumphant now. In fact, if anything, he felt tense and uneasy. As if there was a battle to be fought but he was not quite sure who the enemy might turn out to be.

And yet there was excitement, too. Anticipation. There was something new in the air. He did not know where it would lead. He did not know where he wanted it to lead. Except there was the matter of a kiss that needed to be dealt with. A kiss which she did not remember; and he could not forget.

He put the key in the door and turned it decisively.

Abby came out into the hallway at the sound of the door opening. She had changed into jeans and a threadbare sweater in expectation of shifting furniture around. For a wild moment, she thought perhaps the furniture deliverers had got a key from the porters. When she saw who it was her face fell.

'Oh, it's you.'

Emilio's dark face was unreadable. 'Should I apologise? Or go away and come back later?'

Abby was instantly contrite. 'Of course not. Sorry. I hoped it was the furniture.'

'Ah.' His mouth quirked. 'I take it we are still sitting on the carpet.'

She nodded miserably. 'I thought I'd been so clever. I suppose it was too much to hope for. I'm afraid I've let you down.'

'I doubt that.'

He shrugged himself out of his heavy overcoat and tossed it onto the floor as if it was a dishrag instead of over a thousand pounds worth of exclusive tailoring. His tie, discreetly but unmistakeably silk, followed it. It pooled on top of the coat, gleaming with dull gold and autumn-leaf colours.

'Tell me what happened.'

Abby, who had never seen such elegant clothes on a man, could not take her eyes off the little pile of riches.

He unbuttoned the formal waistcoat. 'Well?'

Abby jumped. There was something extraordinarily intimate about the moment. She tried to concentrate on the subject in hand.

'I—er—'

He freed his cuffs casually and pushed his shirtsleeves up. His forearms were darkly tanned and sinewy. Abby felt her mouth dry.

She averted her eyes hurriedly and reported on her conversation with the hire company. She did not meet his eyes. And she did not look at the powerful forearms, either.

Emilio listened, frowning.

'Very obliging,' he commented when she finished. 'Maybe too obliging.'

'Yes that's what I thought,' admitted Abby, relieved to share her doubts. 'But I can't see what they have to gain by it. Can you?'

He shrugged. 'Maybe nothing. But I think neither you nor I will be here when they arrive.'

'Oh?'

'The whole point of this is to avoid publicity,' he reminded her.

She winced. 'You think that's what this is about?'

'I think it would be wise to take avoiding action, just in case.'

She nodded glumly.

'So what shall we do?'

His eyes flickered for a moment. Then he said, 'Something ordinary. What about a movie and a pizza?'

Abby stared. 'Really?'

'Why not?'

'But you're so—'

'So what?'

'Sophisticated. A movie and a pizza seems a bit down market for you.'

'Oh, you've no idea how down market I can be,' he said with irony.

Abby frowned. There was an edge to the remark which she did not understand.

'Well, if you're sure,' she said uncertainly.

He relented. 'I'm sure. Come on. Let's go and have fun.'

They went to a multiplex. Emilio refused point-blank to go to the latest action adventure, which any of Abby's brothers would have greeted with relish. Instead he offered her a straight choice between a metropolitan comedy, a well-reviewed thriller and tear-jerker.

'But which one do you want to see?' Abby asked.

'Any.'

She chose the thriller. She had seen the comedy and did not want to risk the tear-jerker. She was still feeling a bit tremulous, after leaving the garden flat.

He bought her a bucket of popcorn and the cold drink of her choice. Then he led the way into the theatre and installed her in a seat. Solicitously he helped her out of her jacket and folded it away.

Abby found it all rather ceremonious. Also slightly uncomfortable. When he slid the coat down her arms she gave a little shiver of reaction that was, she told herself, quite uncalled for.

'This is a treat,' she announced, to take her mind off that small betrayal. 'I was expecting to be hauling sofas and chairs around tonight.'

'We'll do that later,' Emilio said, silencing her.

She had thought him stripping off his outer clothes intimate! But that was nothing to this casual assumption that they would be arranging the flat together. As if they shared their lives. As if they were a couple.

For a moment Abby had a blinding sense of rightness.

Then she realised that it was all in her imagination. That was not what Emilio meant at all. She had nearly fallen into a trap he did not even know he had set. She had better be careful.

She burrowed down in the seat and pulled her polo neck up to her ears. She sat quiet as a mouse as the auditorium darkened. She could feel the warmth of his body next to hers; his strength. She could hear his breathing. She could never remember listening to a man's breathing before.

Then the music started. All eyes focused on the screen. Abby risked a sideways glance at Emilio. In silhouette, his profile looked haughty and remote. And yet he was holding her popcorn as if they had done this a thousand times; as if she knew how to breach that haughty remoteness.

Oh, yes it was like being half of a couple. It would have

been quite perfect if the illusion had been true. And if she was the only one who did know how to make that breach.

But Abby was sensible enough to remember that none of it was true. She could easily have dropped her head on his shoulder. And if she had?

Well, he was sophisticated enough to handle it, she thought. He would no doubt respond beautifully. Very courteous. Utterly without meaning. She flexed her shoulders and stared straight ahead.

Very careful, her heart warned.

Emilio could feel her thinking beside him. He just did not know what. It bewildered him.

He had picked up that voluptuous little ripple of reaction when he took her coat. *Yes!* he thought. He waited for her to relax. Surely in the dark she would soften, turn towards him, lean against him, even if only slightly. He was holding her popcorn, for heaven's sake. She could not stay foursquare on to the screen and share a bucket of popcorn.

But she could and she did. From time to time a hand came out of the darkness and rooted in the bucket. But it could have been attached to a robot arm for all the softening there was.

The movie was tautly written. Abby was soon absorbed. She did relax then. At least her shoulders came down from her ears. That did not mean that she turned to him.

What would she do if he took her hand? Emilio wondered savagely. He had not felt so uncertain with a girl since he was a teenager on his first date. Come to that he had *never* felt so uncertain with a girl. Even when he went on his first date he was recognised to be the most attractive boy in his class. His teenage date had known her luck—and her worth, being the choice of Emilio Diz. This awkward English girl could do with some of that confidence.

Ah, but she had never had any confidence, had she? Just that beautiful spontaneity. And a guileless frankness that disarmed him, just when she exasperated him the most.

Emilio slid an arm casually along the back of her seat. It was somewhere between protective and possessive. He mocked himself for the confusion. But he did not take his arm away. Not that it mattered. Abby could not be less aware of it, Emilio thought wryly.

He settled back. It was crazy but he felt more comfortable now that he was cradling the air around her, even if he was not actually touching her. He concentrated on the film at last.

Abby felt the arm go round her seat. Her limbs twitched, as if they were about to stiffen. She fought to stay cool. He probably would not notice, of course. But if he did, he would laugh at her. Anyway, for her own self-respect, she could not sit there twitching with reaction. She was not an untried teenager anymore.

It would be an instinctive thing for him, she told herself. He would not even know he was doing it, probably. Bet he had never been to a movie with a girl without putting his arm round her. It meant nothing to him. It had to mean nothing to her. *Had* to.

Abby reminded herself that she had had lots of experience since the last time Emilio Diz had put his arm round her. Well, some experience. Certainly enough not to fall apart because a man put a casual arm round her. And she was old enough to go to a movie and watch the movie, she told herself crossly.

She did. Eventually.

Unfortunately the admiring reviews had neglected to mention that the thriller was also sad. Torn between outrage and a horrible suspicion that the whole cinema would hear her crying, Abby sat bolt upright and tried to sniff quietly. It was not a success.

The arm closed round her shoulders. He pulled her towards him gently. She resisted for a moment. But only a moment. Then she leaned into the strong warm shoulder and took comfort. She found a handkerchief slipped into her hand.

He must think I'm a *child*, she thought, depressed.

She blotted her eyes, blew her nose and tried to sit up. The arm was suddenly hard around her, not gentle at all. Startled, Abby stopped trying.

They stayed like that until the movie finished. He was clearly someone who liked to see the credits through to the bitter end. He did not let her move until the lights came up. By that time the cinema had nearly emptied.

Abby sniffed and straightened and said the first thing that came into her head. 'You take your movies seriously.'

He looked down at her, his eyes warm. 'I take everything I do seriously. If you don't do it properly, there's no point in wasting time to do it at all.'

Their eyes locked. For a moment Abby thought: he's going to kiss me! She swallowed.

But then the attendant moved into the row behind them, picking up the detritus left by the audience and the moment was gone. Probably all in her imagination, anyway.

She let him help her on with her coat. But she did not meet his eyes again. And all through the pizza and the walk back to the apartment block, she talked brightly about the people she knew and the amusing things they all did together. Nothing personal. Nothing intimate. Nothing that made her feel like an uncertain teenager again.

Emilio let her talk. He was not quite sure what was going on. He mocked himself. With all his experience, he still could not read this woman. She could not be the innocent he remembered. He knew that. But what had she become? Simple, honest and kind as she seemed at some moments? Or the shallow party girl she seemed at other times; like now. Or something more complicated altogether?

She had cried over the movie. She had not seemed like a hard socialite when she turned to him in the darkened cinema. It was only when the lights came up that she had started this social chatter, he realised. And if he touched her, the chatter faltered at once, even now.

One thing his experience made him absolutely certain of.

She was as attracted to him as he was to her. It was there, even when she was not turning to him. She had been totally aware of him in the cinema. She had trembled when he brushed her lips this morning. More than trembled.

Hang on, thought Emilio. Maybe he was wrong about that mutual attraction. Trembling or not, she had not kissed him back this morning.

His experience gave a mocking laugh. Not quite, it pointed out. Not yet.

But she would. Oh, yes, she would.

CHAPTER EIGHT

THE furniture had arrived. It was standing around the main room, still wrapped in muffling sheets of semi-opaque plastic. Abby pulled a face.

'They look like ghosts of furniture, don't they?'

'They look like a lot of work,' said Emilio, slightly taken aback.

'Oh, no. I only got the basics. I hope,' said Abby uneasy now the stuff was actually there, 'that you don't hate my taste too much.'

'Why should I do that?'

'I don't know. I suppose, I didn't really ask you what styles you liked or anything.'

'You read my brief?'

'Yes, but the warehouse didn't exactly run to genuine antiques,' said Abby dryly. 'I had to do the best I could. So I got what I liked.'

Emilio's eyes danced suddenly. 'Then let's see how far apart we are, shall we?'

He produced a Swiss Army knife and slit the plastic covering the largest piece of furniture. After a moment's hesitation, Abby followed suit.

It took them an hour to strip off the coverings and put the stuff in place. Emilio stood back and surveyed the drawing room. Abby folded her arms round herself, horribly anxious now it was done.

'Comfortable,' he pronounced at last. 'Welcoming. I like that big table lamp.'

Her heart sank. 'Only the lamp?'

'No.'

Emilio did not quite know what he was feeling. The family

house in BA was full of intricately carved furniture and carefully displayed works of art. The Spanish place still had the antiques he had bought with it. His apartment in New York was minimalist and functional. He had never had deep winged chairs before. Or Persian rugs. Or cushions. So many cushions, in such different sizes; and in such a kaleidoscope of colours and design.

He said carefully, 'It's all a lot more solid than I'm used to. But I like it, I think. Feels like a home. It will just take a bit of time for it to feel like *my* home.'

She had to be content with that.

He did not comment at all on the furniture she had selected for her own room. Abby was grateful. It was the only area in which the warehouse had let her down. She had picked out a plain bed, halfway between single and double size, with a coordinating chest. But what arrived was very different.

For one thing the bed was shaped like a sleigh and gleamed with cherrywood. For another, it was enormous. The chest was equally substantial. Her small supply of sweaters and underclothes would be lost in it. Just as she would be lost in that great bed.

Emilio said nothing, as he helped push it into place though, except, 'Did you get bed linen?'

'Not from the warehouse,' said Abby, briskly practical. It was her only defence against embarrassment but it seemed to work. 'I bought some, along with a duvet and a couple of pillows.'

The duvet would be big enough, just about, but she was not sure about the sheets. She might have to raid the ones she had bought for Emilio's bed and return the others tomorrow. Blast it.

'I got some cutlery and some basic china, too. Plain white. Hope that's all right.'

'Fine,' he said indifferently.

Abby shook her head. 'You know you're the most surprising millionaire I've ever met.'

'Oh? Why?'

'You really don't care about all this stuff, do you?' She gestured round the room.

He laughed. 'I don't have big emotional relationships with tables and chairs, no.'

Abby's eyes narrowed. 'What about pizza and a movie?'

'Oh, sure, I have an emotional relationship with pizza. Show me the man who doesn't.'

'That's not what I meant.'

'So explain.'

Abby was trying to. 'My father knows people who are rich. I mean very rich. I've known them all my life. They *do* care about tables and chairs. Everything has to be the best. It all has to show everyone that they can afford the best.' She smiled suddenly. 'I don't know one of them who would have taken me to a movie, tonight. A Michelin-starred restaurant would be more in their line.'

The dark eyes were very grave. 'Is that a problem?'

'What?' She did not understand.

'Do you want a—shall we say, more conventional—millionaire?'

Abby shook her head violently. 'No, of course not.'

And then heard what she had said.

'Not that I mean I want you. I mean, I don't *not*—I mean, I never thought—I, oh, help!'

He had been listening with deep appreciation. Now he helped her out of her misery.

'It wasn't a fair question.'

Abby pressed a hand to a hot cheek and glared at him. 'No, it wasn't.'

'But irresistible,' he murmured.

She was so furious she forgot she was embarrassed. 'And that's not fair, either. I'm grateful to you for helping me out like this. But that doesn't mean you can just wind me up whenever you feel like a good laugh.'

'I apologise.'

'I'm not here for your entertainment.'

'I *apologise.*'

It took the wind out of her sails, rather.

'Oh, all right,' she said not very graciously.

Emilio looked at her thoughtfully. 'You're very sensitive.'

Abby sighed and told the truth. 'That's just it. I'm not.' She shook her head. 'Well, not usually. If you have four brothers you sort of get immune to teasing. Families are a great training for life's assault course.'

He looked thunderstruck. 'Families! Damn!'

'What?'

'I've got a call I need to make. I forgot.' He looked at his watch. 'Maybe it's not too late.'

Abby realised suddenly that she was intruding on his privacy. She jumped to her feet.

'I'll go and make some coffee. I bought that, too.'

She did. But not before she heard him say into the phone in Spanish, 'Isabel? Sorry love, things came up. Now tell me what's really wrong. And no more nonsense about garbage collection.'

It sounded as if they were incredibly close. Abby winced, excluded. Then promptly told herself that she had no right to feel excluded. It was not as if they were living together, for heaven's sake. They were just two ships who should have passed in the night. OK, they had ended up in harbour together because of storms at sea. But as soon as the storms blew over, they would steam on their way. Going in different directions, no doubt.

You have no rights in him, she told herself. And sharing his flat isn't going to give you any.

Not, of course, that she wanted any. Heck, she had only known him for a day. Well, a day and a few intense hours nine years ago, of which she was not going to remind him. Of course, she did not want any rights in him. Isabel, whoever she was, was welcome to him.

He finished his phone call and followed her out to the kitchen.

'Sorry about that. Domestic crisis in the offing.'

'Oh.' Abby's tone was not encouraging.

Emilio did not appear to notice. 'What do you do with a nine-year-old who says he's not going back to school? Then locks himself in his room to prove his point.'

In the act of pouring coffee, Abby froze. A nine-year-old? He had a child?

Why had she not thought of that? Why had she not remembered that the sophisticated set he belonged to did not necessarily marry? They just paired up when they felt like it and parted when they were bored.

She knew Isabel was not his wife. He had explained very carefully why he could not afford a wife. Had Isabel had to be content with being the mother of his child then?

It wouldn't do for me, thought Abby. That little clutch of children's books in the cupboard in her room seemed to mock her. She made a small sound of distress.

'What is it?' said Emilio.

She couldn't say, 'I've just had another sophistication failure.' She finished pouring the coffee.

She shrugged, making very good display of indifference. 'I don't know anything about nine-year-olds. My brothers are all older than I am.'

'Well, take it from me they're a pain in the butt,' he said grimly. 'Especially when they're an only child of a doting single mother.'

Abby was horribly shocked. She struggled to restrain it but her every instinct screamed at her to protest, even if it made him laugh at her unworldliness. She held on to it, but only just.

Emilio did not notice. He was frowning, clearly impatient. 'The trouble is she was much too young when he was born. As a result he is wilful as sin. And, of course, spoilt.'

The sophistication failure was total. 'Does he—do they—live with you?' she asked in a strangled voice.

'Yes and no. There's a family house but Isabel and Daniel have their own apartment.'

It sounded bleak.

'Maybe that's the problem.' It burst out of her. She could not help it.

Emilio noticed her reaction something at last. He stared. 'What?'

She turned away. 'I'm sorry. I shouldn't have said that.'

'No, go on. You clearly have something to say.'

'It's nothing to do with me.'

'Don't let that stop you now.'

'Fine,' she said, goaded. 'You asked for it. Maybe if his father didn't live in another part of the house and take off all round the world all the time, the child would not refuse to go to school. Or,' she added savagely, 'be a pain in the butt.'

'His father!'

Abby caught herself. 'I know it's none of my business. But you did ask.'

'His *father?*'

How could he look so outraged? Did he think bringing up a child he sired was nothing to do with him?

Abby's temper stirred. 'It takes more than an exchange of body fluids to be a proper father,' she flashed.

Emilio's head went back as if she had hit him.

'It does indeed,' he said softly.

Abby heard the note of danger. She said hastily, 'I shouldn't have said that. If you want to keep one jump ahead of real relationships, it's up to you.'

He gave her a glittering smile. It did not get anywhere near his eyes.

'Oh, why not? If you think I'm a cold-hearted playboy, why not go ahead and say it.'

Something very wrong here, thought Abby.

'I didn't say that.'

'I think you did.'

Very wrong.

'If I've upset you—' she began stiffly.

He gave a bark of laughter. 'Oh, what's to upset? You've just accused me of neglecting my son, insulting his mother and abandoning the pair of them whenever I feel like it. What's wrong with that?'

Abby realised she had made a mistake. A big mistake. Much, much bigger than a simple sophistication failure.

She said, 'He's not your son, is he?'

Emilio looked at her in silence for a moment. A muscle worked in his jaw.

Then he said curtly, 'No.'

Abby wanted to die. How could she have been so stupid? That was what came of trying so hard to prove that she knew the score!

She said wretchedly, 'Who is he?'

'My sister Isabel's son.'

'And—his father?'

Emilio's mouth thinned. 'If I knew for certain who he was, I'd probably kill him.'

'What?'

He sighed angrily. 'Now you think I'm a potential murderer. No, Abby, not literally. Moral delinquent, though I am, I don't kill people.'

She winced.

'But I would have made him face his responsibilities years ago, by force if necessary.' He flung her a challenging look. 'And I make no apology for that.'

Abby swallowed. She wanted to sink into the ground. 'But you don't know who he is?'

The challenging look subsided. He looked tired suddenly.

'Bebel won't say. So I do the best I can as a substitute father. To be honest, it's not a great best.'

Abby looked at him and made a discovery. He minded.

She said forgot her horrible gaffe. She said gently, 'What do you think you do wrong?'

He turned away. 'Oh, everything. I'm the only one to provide discipline, you see. That makes me an ogre. Bebel says he's afraid of me. She may be right.'

'*Afraid* of you?'

'Lots of people are,' said Emilio in a hard voice. 'There's a whole floor of them at Traynor for example. And Bebel has sometimes said that she wouldn't have gone off the rails if she had not been too afraid to talk to me when she was a teenager.'

Abby heard self-reproach. And more than self-reproach, a bleak loneliness that touched her to the heart. She nearly put out a hand to touch him. In the end she did not quite dare. Not after what she had just accused him of.

She said to his back, 'Why was she afraid of you? Were you a substitute father for your sister as well, then?'

Emilio turned round. She could not read anything in his expression at all.

'I was the breadwinner,' he said uncommunicatively.

Abby hesitated. 'When did your sister—?'

But he flung up a hand. 'It's too late to give you a rundown on my family history. I have a long day tomorrow.'

Abby was wretchedly torn. She wanted to apologise. To say that she did not think he was a cold-hearted playboy, that she had just been rocked off balance for a moment. But if she did that, she had to say why she had reacted so strongly. And she did not know. Except that for a moment she had felt almost jealous of the abandoned Isabel. And, of course, she could not say that.

So in the end, she said nothing.

She stood up. 'OK. I'll see you in the morning, then.'

But in the morning, he was gone.

The next couple of days were extraordinary for Abby. At home she rattled around in the newly furnished flat like an unwanted extra on an empty film set. At work, no matter how hard she tried to devote herself to the tasks in her in-tray, she could not quite get rid of the idea that people were watching her.

'Have I suddenly grown two heads?' she asked Molly di Perretti.

Molly shook her head. 'On the contrary. You tamed the beast.'

'What?'

'Remember Sam saying that Traynors were going to sack us? Well, the big cheese changed his mind. Everyone seems to think that was down to you.'

'Oh,' said Abby.

'And not because of the blue blood, either. Diz is known for his hostility to the ruling classes.'

'Oh,' said Abby again in quite a different voice. Her heart sank.

'So turquoise hair maybe. Blue blood no.' Molly quirked an eyebrow. 'Has he called you yet?'

'No,' said Abby honestly.

'He will.'

It seemed the whole office was waiting for him to do just that. They asked her when they met her by the water fountain. They sent her messages on the internal e-mail. They quizzed Fran on the switchboard.

When Emilio Diz did not call, the staff of C&C were first confused, then indignant. To comfort Abby for her supposed disappointment they bombarded her with reasons that she was better off without him.

'They called him the Romeo of the circuit,' said Sam, passing by her desk with a consoling pat. 'There was a scandal in Paris with a couple of young fans.'

The ancient press cutting arrived in her mailbox later that day.

Abby read it with distaste and then wiped it. It would have been a lot more satisfying to tear it into pieces but she hit the Delete button with enough force to send the End key next to it ricocheting off the keyboard.

'Keep your hair on,' said Molly. She chased the errant key under a nearby desk and emerged triumphant. 'There are plenty more fish in the sea. Anyway, clever men are hell.'

A whole portfolio of press cuttings attesting to Emilio's brilliant business brain was the next message to arrive in Abby's e-mail.

She read those with less distaste but more alarm. They talked about a lot more than his brilliance. They were full of his ruthlessness, as well.

And she remembered Felipe Montijo saying, 'Emilio plays to win.'

Yet this was the man who was a father substitute to his family. The man who had offered Abby sanctuary when she desperately needed it. The man who had put his arm round her and given her a handkerchief when she cried. It didn't add up.

Emilio himself was silent. There was a message from his office on the answering machine in the flat. Emilio it seemed had gone to Zurich first, then on to Frankfurt. After that he was probably going to his sports complex in Spain. He would be in touch when his plans were clear.

But if Emilio was uncommunicative, Abby's family were in touch on an hourly basis, it seemed. Will in northern India had tried to call Abby. Justine had taken the opportunity to tell him his sister had moved out. She had no idea where but it was about time the girl stood on her own two feet. Will cut her off and rang Abby at work.

'What has that poisonous witch done to you?' said Will, who had overlapped with Justine for three volcanic days before he went back to his job of leading adventure holidays.

Abby told him what had happened.

'And Dad doesn't know?'

'What can I tell him?'

'How about the truth?' suggested Will. 'You didn't try to

put the boot in. She did. If Dad decides she's surplus to requirement, she only has herself to blame.'

'But I—'

'You reap what you sow. That goes for Justine, too.'

He was not a great forgiver, thought Abby.

She said with finality, 'I'm not interfering in their marriage.'

'So what are you going to do? Sleep on other people's floors and tell lies about it?'

Abby laughed. 'Oh, come on, Will. It's not the end of the world. Lots of people share flats.'

'Fine. Who are you sharing with?'

'It's—um—quite temporary,' said Abby hastily. 'Haven't made up my mind what to do long term yet.'

'See, you *are* telling lies. Even to yourself. What do the boys say? Or haven't you told them, either?'

'No,' admitted Abby.

'Huh,' said Will. 'Then I will.'

Which, of course, meant that Rob and Nick rang from Australia, full of generous indignation and offers of the plane fare to join them on their round-the-world sail. Abby declined. Sandy, test flying the new generation of helicopters in the Mojave Desert, was not slow to follow.

'She can't turn you out,' said Sandy, always the most level-headed of her brothers, in spite of his job. 'It's not her house. Go and see the lawyers.'

The only one who did not call was their father. Abby was relieved. She had told her brothers that she was going to keep silent and let her father work his own stuff out with Justine. But if her father actually called, she was not sure that she could withstand the temptation to tell him the whole truth.

So she kept herself busy. She also went out a lot. The flat was too big and too empty, in spite of its fine new complement of furniture. Her ears were constantly on the stretch for Emilio's key in the door or his voice from the other room.

Abby knew it was crazy. You could not miss someone

after so short a space of time. But she did and there was nothing she could do about it. So she accepted every invitation or offer of extra work that came her way.

'That hair has turned you into a party girl at last,' teased Molly, air-brushing glitter powder down her cleavage with a lavish hand.

It was Saturday night and they were in Molly's bedroom. They were going to the wrap party of the newest Brit flick. The production company was Molly's client but Abby had worked on the account, too. They had both received invitations shaped like witches' hats. It was a mayhem and magic movie.

Abby, going with the theme, was wearing slim ankle-length black, with sumptuous mediaeval sleeves that she had sat up until two that morning to make. Well, it was better than tossing and turning in that too large bed, wondering where Emilio was. She had lined the sleeves with turquoise to match her hair. Her mouth and her fingernails were a voluptuously threatening purple. She was now applying black eyeliner.

'You look gorgeous,' said Molly generously. 'You're a really talented dressmaker when you put your mind to it, aren't you?'

Abby grinned. 'Needs must. It was that or the Oxfam shop when I was growing up.'

Molly was shocked. 'But I thought—'

Abby put the eyeliner away. She debated between a silver moon and a star beauty spot.

'You thought earls had the stuff by the barrel load,' she agreed absently.

'They don't?'

'It comes in. And it goes out. Through the roof usually. My father actually earns quite a lot, I suppose. But the house just eats it. Any designer dresses I had were designed by me.'

'Well, you're as good as Ravi any day.'

'At least I can get in and out of this without the help of a personal trainer,' said Abby darkly, remembering the shoe-lace-backed effort had put her in Emilio's hands.

She gave a little shiver of reaction.

Not a good idea. She was going to a party, for heaven's sake. She should be looking forward to the people she would meet there. Not thinking about a man she couldn't have.

She picked up the crescent moon and held it against the corner of her mouth. 'What do you think? Or the star?'

'Go for both,' advised Molly. 'That is not a dress which deserves moderation.'

In addition to the sleeves, it was slit to the thigh. You did not see until Abby started to move. It revealed the entire length of one sheer black leg.

'Wow,' Molly said, when she first saw it.

Now Abby pointed her toe sideways. She watched the way the material fell away and pulled a face.

'It wasn't meant to be quite so provocative. But when I made it up, I couldn't move except in a sort of a geisha shuffle. So I kept on unpicking until I could take a reasonable stride. And this is the result.'

'Some result,' said Molly enthusiastically. 'I'd say fate is pointing you in the direction of some serious bad behaviour.'

Abby looked alarmed.

'Go with the flow,' Molly advised. 'You're due some fun. You've worked like a dog all week. Live a little.'

So as soon as they got to the party, Molly cornered the heaviest-lidded, most laid-back cameraman and said, 'That is your publicist Lady Abigail Templeton Burke. She's been working hard for you. Take her onto the dance floor and say thank you nicely.'

He did.

The music was heavy with rhythm and much too loud to talk. So Abby bopped cheerfully on the dance floor with a series of men whose names she never caught. The producer took her off for a plate of spicy nibbles and a photo opportunity with the film's star. A young journalist she knew brought her a drink and asked her some questions she could not hear. She smiled and nodded endorsement of whatever he was saying and let him take her picture.

'Thank God for you,' he said with feeling. 'No one else here knows I'm alive.'

Abby remembered that feeling of invisibility. 'Come and dance with me,' she offered.

He seized her gratefully. 'Rescue service provided by the Fab Ab. Thanks, babe.'

'Just don't expect me to wear a barrel of brandy round my neck,' said Abby, laughing.

He was not a good dancer but he was not a groper, either. When Abby detached herself, he let her go with a smile.

She went to the ladies' room and repaired her make-up. Then she danced some more. Drank a little. Received several compliments on her dress.

When the party had thinned out to the hard core, Molly said, 'We're going on with Billy. Coming?'

Abby thought of the empty flat and said yes, before she had even asked who Billy was or where they were going on to.

It was someone's house in a part of London she did not know. She sat on the knee of someone else she didn't know in the car going there. A lot of the laughter was drunken. A lot of the conversation was infantile. By the time she got there Abby knew it was a mistake.

She said so to Molly.

'Oh, come. Lighten up. I thought you were breaking out of that good girl image. Don't be scared.'

'I'm not scared. I just haven't drunk enough to play the five-year-old,' said Abby tartly.

'Then have some more champagne.'

But even the empty flat was preferable to being groped by middle-aged men who wanted to believe they were still eighteen.

'I'm going,' said Abby. She dialled up her favourite cab company on her mobile phone.

The journalist who had taken her picture came down the stairs. His eyes lit up when he saw her.

'Hey, babe. Come and party.'

She shook her head, talking to the cab company. Then she disconnected and gave him a conspiratorial grin. 'Find your rescue somewhere else this time.'

'Abby's going,' said Molly with an expression of disgust.

'Really? So should I, I guess. Can I share your cab?'

'OK,' said Abby.

She thought he was probably new in the job. She had met him this week for the first time. Then bumped into him twice more. He was always looking round as if he did not quite know what to do next. She understood that feeling.

He held the door open for her and gave the cab driver instructions. Then he got in beside her.

'Wow. Riding through the town with the Fab Ab,' he said.

She looked at him in disbelief. Surely no one could be that naive. She tipped her head against the back of the seat and closed her eyes.

He did not take the hint. 'You look tired. Heavy week?'

'I've been out and about,' she agreed.

'Feeling neglected?'

She opened her eyes and looked at him warily. Had he heard about Justine throwing her out?

'Why should I?'

'Well, boyfriend away—all alone in your new home—can't be easy.'

Abby sat bolt upright. 'What are you talking about?'

He gave her a smile which she suddenly saw was not naive at all. 'Well, you wouldn't have been at that party on your own if the boyfriend was in town, would you? Or not unless you'd had a row.' He did not exactly lick his pencil and make notes but the feeling was there. 'Have you fallen out with Emilio already?'

'No,'

'He has that reputation, of course. Minimal sticking power. He never sticks with the ladies for long. But it's supposed to be great while it lasts. How is it so far?'

Abby did not answer. She went on not answering throughout the rest of the nightmare drive through the empty streets. It can only have been twenty minutes or so but it felt like a lifetime.

It was only when the minicab drew up outside her building that she realised the journalist had never asked for her address. So he must already have known it. Her blood ran cold at the thought.

She slid out without saying goodnight. It cost her a lot not to pelt for safety the moment she was out of the car. But Abby had her pride. Turquoise head high, she stalked into the entrance hall. She did not look back.

But once inside, she gave way to the shaking inside.

What have I done? she thought. What on earth have I done?

Federico's problem was more complicated than Emilio expected. Even after a couple of days, he was not really sure that he knew what the difficulty was. All Federico would say was that he needed to take stock.

'What do you mean, take stock?'

'Think about where I'm going. And whether I want to go there.'

'Oh, that old thing,' said Emilio ironically. 'Don't take too long. You may find you've already gone further than you thought.'

He did not say that he was taking stock himself, after that nasty little scene with Abby. Where have I got to? he thought. He had been furious—and, if he were honest, furiously hurt—when she threw her accusations at him.

Most he could throw off. A lot he could ascribe to years

of press scandal and, even more, to the sheltered life she had undoubtedly led. But—

She had said, 'If you want to keep one jump ahead of real relationships, it's up to you.'

It had shocked him at the time. But then he had been angry with her, angry that she could think such things of him. But now, cooler, days later, it still nagged away at him. He had no idea why.

'...one jump ahead of real relationships...'

It was nonsense. Of course it was nonsense.

And he was certainly not going to discuss it with Federico, who was showing signs of getting altogether too open to nonsense.

So Emilio gave his brother some curt advice to sharpen up his ideas and went to check on some of his other European investments.

He ended in Madrid at his European headquarters. He nearly went to London. But the Spanish company needed his attention in the way Traynor didn't at the moment. And anyway he wanted to go to the Palacio Azul. He had not been there for months and he wanted to make sure it was ready.

He did not ask himself ready for what.

He did not speak to Abby while he was travelling. It was not as if they were lovers, after all, he told himself. He did not have to show her that he was not a cold-hearted playboy. She either believed him or she didn't. He had nothing to prove.

He did, in fact, telephone the apartment several times but the answering machine was always on. He rang off, not leaving a message. If he were honest, he did not know what message to leave.

The evening at the movie theatre had shaken him. He had not felt so aware of a woman in years. But it was much more than sexual awareness. When she burned herself he wanted to heal her. When she was tired he wanted to take her burdens and carry them for her. And he had found himself starting to tell her about Bebel, as he had never told anyone, man or woman. Until last week he would have called it disloyal and he was never disloyal to his family. But telling Abby his family's secrets did not feel like disloyalty. It felt natural.

I'm getting in very deep, thought Emilio. How much deeper can I go without telling her that we've met before? Hell, that we've kissed before. And that I've never forgotten.

He avoided London while he tried to get his head around it.

He went to the Palacio Azul and prowled restlessly round the house. Later he sat on the terrace in the thin February sunshine and looked across the valley at the Andalucian mountains. His glass of wine dangled forgotten in his hand. The hillside in front of the house was studded with olive and almond trees, eucalyptus and old fruit trees that would be in flower in just a few weeks. There was a chill in the air, especially in the morning, but there was still the scent of dust and herbs and living wood that he always associated with his secret hillside.

He looked down at his wine. He wanted Abby here. He wanted her to argue with. He wanted to share the spring with her.

He knew that the girl who had lectured him about roses would love all the exuberant blossom. With its carpet of poppies and cowslips and blue borage turning the orchards into something out of a mediaeval Book of Hours. He wanted to walk her among the white blossom of the cherry trees. He wanted to take her to the magical white villages that the region was famous for.

Maybe here he would be able to tell her about that night nine years ago. Maybe here he could tell her that he had never forgotten it. And that he had known who she was the moment he saw her

Maybe here, she would forgive him. Forgive him for rejecting her then. And for holding out on her now. She was

a passionate fighter but she had a heart. And there was always
that sizzling attraction.

Maybe she would listen to her instincts if he brought her
to his enchanted mountaintop.

Maybe.

CHAPTER NINE

EMILIO flew back from Granada to Madrid on Monday. All through the journey he kept breaking into a smile.

The flight attendant was impressed. Not many celebrities were as accommodating as Emilio Diz. He was even charming when the landing was delayed.

She would have been astonished if she had seen the trepidation with which his arrival was awaited in the Madrid office.

'He's going to be so mad,' said his Spanish PA, her face ashen. 'Can't we do something?'

'Like what?' said the chief executive officer of Diz España. He was more composed but no less concerned. 'I've never even heard of the woman.'

So when Emilio walked in, he found an office in the grip of cathedral gloom.

'What's wrong?' he said, used to a cheerful buzz.

'Press cuttings,' said his faithful PA of ten years.

She thrust a folder at him and almost ran out of his room.

Emilio turned it over. It was not thick. Only one press cutting. He judged. With a sense of foreboding he opened it.

There was a colour photograph of Abby. She had clearly posed for it. She was raising a champagne flute to the photographer. But it was not the champagne that Emilio looked at. She had a half moon curved sexily round the corner of her pouting mouth. Her nails were the same colour as her hair. And her skirt was split to the waist.

For a moment Emilio quite simply did not believe it. Then he looked at the partying figures in the background, the tell-tale shaky eyeliner above her right eye. Oh, yes, this was no fake.

He felt his rage ignite. He went physically hot with it. Then deadly cold.

He applied himself to the text of the article.

Monday was a thin day for Tracy's Town Gossip. So Abby got the full treatment. And so did he.

The Fab Ab Hits The Scene.

Lovely Lady Abigail Templeton Burke, snapped at the Ariadne Films' Moon Maid party.

The Fab Ab, 25, recently hit the headlines when she dumped Deor Spiro of boy band Hackney Wick. Deor said he had no idea why the daughter of the Earl of Nunnington went off him. Now Tracy, exclusively, can give him a clue.

Gorgeous Abby, who works at PR firm Culp and Christopher, has been changing her image. First her hair. Then her gear. And her colleagues are all asking why.

They're answering, too. The word on the street is that the Fab Ab has a new squeeze. She disappeared from her trendy basement flat in SE11, to reappear in even more upmarket SW3. Tracy hears that only last week the lovely ex deb was out looking for film set furniture to glam up her new pad.

Or is it hers? Templeton Burke is not among the listed owners in swish St. Francis Place. A listed resident on the floor where the Fab Ab has been seen getting out of the lift, however, is Emilio Diz.

Dishy Diz, readers will remember, has broken more hearts than Tracy has had hot dinners. Once an international tennis star, then a software tycoon, these days Emilio is into property. Some of the property he has checked out in recent years is movie star Callie Dean, heiress Florita Guzman, and socialite Rosanna Sanchez Montijo—see photographs.

But Emilio was not around this weekend. His office didn't know where to get in touch with him when Tracy rang. Is that why the Fab Ab went partying alone?

*Emilio's loss is some lucky guy's gain. Check those legs.
Go for it, Ab!*

Emilio flung the folder away from him.

In the outer office everyone heard the squashy sound as the cardboard hit the wall. They all winced.

The door to the inner sanctum was flung open. Emilio appeared at it. Every single person in the room took one look at his black frown and grouped around the PA's desk for mutual support.

But when he spoke it was with low-voiced control.

'Beatriz, get me on the next to flight to London. There's something I have to deal with.'

He closed the door with a studied care that was somehow more alarming than violence.

Everyone let out a shaky breath.

'Well at least he didn't say *someone*,' said the post boy practically.

'But that's what he meant,' said the PA, dialling. 'Poor woman. She doesn't know what she's let herself in for.'

'Poor woman indeed. I hope she's not in love with him,' said her tender-hearted assistant. 'She's really blown it now. He'll never look at her after this.'

Abby stared at the page of newsprint as if she had forgotten how to read English.

'That's disgusting,' she said.

Molly di Perretti, unusually subdued, brought her coffee.

'Is it true?'

'What?'

'That you're living with Diz? Is that why he didn't call?'

Abby looked up from the newspaper clipping. 'Well—it's complicated,' she hedged. 'But basically I suppose—yes, I am.'

'You're *living* with him? You?'

'I'm old enough,' said Abby defensively.

'And six months ago you still had straw in your hair.' Molly sounded despairing. 'Oh, hell, this is all my fault. I should never have told you to go out and party.'

'You didn't. And anyway, I do what I want, not what anyone tells me,' said Abby, revolted.

'So why did you get mixed up with Emilio Diz? You know what he's like. His sort of guy is in and out of this place all the time. They're good fun and they're usually great in bed. But they're not your type.'

Abby bridled. 'What do you mean, not my type? Why should I turn up my nose at a man just because he's great in bed?'

'Oh, Abby.' There were tears in Molly's eyes. 'You're a commitment junky. You're always running round doing stuff for your family. Hell, even for your godchildren. You've never loved 'em and left 'em in your life.'

'But I've changed—'

'Not that much. It takes more than turquoise hair to turn a home-maker into a brazen hussy,' said Molly, bravely attempting a joke.

'I thought I'd learned so much.'

'You have. But you're still human. And when it comes to heartlessness, you ain't in the same class as Emilio Diz. Take it from an expert.'

A sudden suspicion occurred to Abby. 'Do you know him?'

'No,' said Molly. 'But I've been a groupie and I've been a publicist. I know guys like him. Believe me, I know what I'm talking about. Get out before he takes you to pieces.'

Abby looked down at the newspaper cutting.

'After this piece of nastiness, I'm probably not going to get the choice to do anything else,' she said.

She tried to call him. But the number on his business card just transferred her to his message service and she did not know what to say to it. So she hung up.

Abby was worried. A couple of journalists tried to get in

touch with her at C&C. Fortunately she had already put up the barrier of voice mail but it was not a comfortable feeling. And if they went chasing Emilio with more success than she had had... It did not bear thinking about.

'Relax,' said Molly, seeing her agitation. 'He's had more experience at this game than you have. He'll handle it with one hand tied behind his back.'

'Yes, but I should have been more careful. He shouldn't *have* to handle it.'

Molly shrugged. 'Probably won't give a toss.' She gave a shadow of her old grin. 'He's not a sensitive flower like you.'

'You could be right,' admitted Abby.

But she was doubtful. Her instincts told her that Emilio would be mad as fire. And that he had every right to be.

So she was not surprised when she got back to the flat that night to find an overnight case in the hall and a dark overcoat thrown over the end of the drawing room sofa.

The drawing room itself was empty. So was the kitchen. So was the dining room.

Abby stood in the corridor and looked at the closed door of the master bedroom.

'Emilio?' she called.

She was quite proud of the way she sounded. Friendly, confident, no trace of guilt. Yes, it wasn't a bad effort at standing her present feelings on their head. She had never felt more miserably responsible in her life.

It was wasted. There was no reply. Perhaps he had come in and gone out again.

She prowled round the sitting room for clues. No message on the desk. But—yes, there were his keys on the console table under the lamp.

She went back to the hallway and called again, louder.

The door of the master suite slammed open. And Abby's stomach did a tap dance through the floor. She stood rock-still, her mouth open.

Emilio had been in the shower. He had a towel round his waist. He was rubbing his hair vigorously with another.

His skin was golden. His muscles were startling. And his expression was volcanic.

'Oh, Lord,' said Abby involuntarily.

He stopped towelling his hair. His dark eyes stayed molten, though.

'Well, well. The Fab Ab.'

Abby flinched. 'Don't call me that.'

'Why not? It seems to be your preferred label.' His accent was very strong.

'Of course it isn't.'

'No? Then maybe it's what in the business world we call your unique selling point.'

Abby was getting angry in her turn. 'There's no need to be nasty. I'm as unhappy about that article as you are. But you're at least as much responsible as I am. If you weren't Dishy Diz the Celebrity Slayer they would never have mentioned you. And they might have left me alone, too.'

'Are you saying it's my fault?' He sounded outraged.

'No, of course not. But you're not exactly low profile, are you?'

'I,' he said with deadly precision, 'don't pose for cameras with my clothes falling off.'

That hurt. Because, of course, she had posed for that photograph and it must be perfectly obvious that she had.

So she fought on the other front. 'My dress wasn't falling off. It was perfectly respectable.'

'There was not enough of it to be perfectly respectable,' Emilio said crushingly.

She flushed. But she was not going to let him get away with that. She had enough to apologise for. She could not afford to let unfounded accusations go unchallenged.

'You're very puritanical for someone who dates three women at a time,' she snapped.

'Three—' He looked thunderstruck.

'Callie Dean, some heiress or other and Rosanna Montijo,' she quoted at him.

'You believe that nonsense?'

'Why not? You did.'

He glared but for a moment, it seemed, she had silenced him. Then, to Abby's dismay, he returned to the one point on which she knew her defence was shaky.

'So why did you give them a picture?'

Abby bit her lip. 'I didn't think—'

'I can believe that.'

She raised her voice. 'I didn't think he would use it like that. I thought it would probably get lost on the cutting room floor. At the most, I expected him to put it in a montage of pictures of the party. You know the sort of thing. Ermentrude Gutbucket enjoying a joke with the Shah of Euphoria. That sort of thing.'

He regarded at her unflatteringly. 'Why? You weren't enjoying a joke with anyone. Except the reptile who took the picture I guess.'

Abby sucked her teeth. She could not deny it. 'Sorry,' she said in a small voice.

'Who was he?'

She shrugged.

'Did you know him?'

'Sort of,' she muttered.

'Sort of? What does that mean?'

'I thought he was a friend.'

He gave an exasperated sigh. 'Journalists don't have friends. They have angles.'

'What?'

'Think about it,' he advised.

He pushed a hand through his damp hair. The fury seemed to have died down, at least for the moment. Abby saw it with relief.

'I haven't talked to any journalist today. They've all been calling but I kept my head down.'

'Well, thank God for that, at least,'

She looked at him with dislike. 'Everyone at C&C,' she said pointedly, 'was very sympathetic. Very supportive.'

'Of course they were. It's in their interest.'

Angry tears leaped to her eyes.

'They've been *kind*,' she protested. 'They don't need to be. I'm still new. They only employ me because they need someone to run errands.'

'I know why they employ you,' Emilio said coldly. 'Turquoise hair and a title.'

There was a shattered silence.

'You are hateful,' Abby whispered.

She turned her back on him and stormed back into the kitchen. The tears were starting to fall. She couldn't bear it if Emilio saw that. She could not afford any weakness in front of him.

She tore off some kitchen roll and blew her nose vigorously. Then she blotted her eyes with care. No tell-tale mascara smudges for her.

She banged about the kitchen loudly. That ought to tell him that she was making coffee, just as she always did. And she did not give two hoots for him and his criticism. If she had known how, she would have whistled something upbeat to show how little she cared. But she had never mastered whistling and she did not want to risk a song. Her voice might break.

Eventually, the water boiled. Abby made the coffee she did not want and sat down at the kitchen table. To all appearances she was lost in thought. But she kept one eye on the door, half wary, half belligerent.

She did not have long to wait.

Emilio had got rid of the towel but he had not managed to replace it with much. Just a pair of black jeans. His feet were bare and so was his golden, gleaming torso.

Abby was startled. This, she thought, was not fair. She

gulped audibly and swallowed some scalding coffee by mistake.

'*Ow.*'

He did not notice. He came and sat opposite her. He seemed to have got rid of his temper, too. At least, his eyes were not smouldering anymore. In fact she could not read any expression at all in the dark depths.

'OK,' he said.

As if he was in the middle of one of his business negotiations, Abby thought resentfully.

'We have a situation here. I can contain it but I need to know the truth. I want you to tell me what else you've told this guy.'

Abby forgot her blistered palate in her indignation. 'Nothing. I told him *nothing.*'

'So how did he find out about the furniture?'

She spread her hands helplessly. 'Pass.'

He looked at her narrowly. 'You're taking this very lightly, for a girl who was willing to sleep in a student dive to avoid publicity.'

Abby studied the tabletop. 'It's not the same thing.'

'No? How is it different?'

She struggled to explain. 'Well, my father's wife hasn't got anything to do with it, for one thing. If anyone gets hurt it's just me. My family isn't involved.'

He drew a breath as sharp as if he had run a splinter under his nail.

But when he spoke, his tone was even. 'No,' he said pleasantly. 'They're not. I am.'

Abby looked up so fast, her spine jerked.

'Why should you care?'

His eyes were almost black. 'Is that a polite way of telling me I don't count?'

She had been wrong. He had not got rid of his temper. It was still there. Oh, it was banked down and he was not letting it show. But underneath he was furious.

Abby felt as if she was being suffocated by that fury. All the more so because she did not understand it.

She said, in a bewildered voice, 'You can't be bothered about that sort of gossip.'

'I have a family, too.'

'Then they must be used to it,' she said hardily. 'The columnists have been linking your name with dozens of women for years. I've got a file full of your old press clippings at the office.'

The moment she said it she knew she shouldn't have done. His eyes narrowed until they were almost invisible under the fierce brows.

'You—have—what?'

The oxygen supply reduced even further.

She tried to explain. 'The guys at C&C have been sending them to me.'

'So you have been researching me?' His accent was like a machine gun. 'Is this an orchestrated campaign?'

'No,' gasped Abby, appalled.

He ignored that. 'Can I look forward to another episode tomorrow?'

She leaped to her feet. *'No!'*

He looked her up and down. Slowly. Insultingly.

'I should warn you. You've picked the wrong man for games.'

Abby huddled her arms round herself. 'Oh, I know that,' she said bitterly. 'Any games you play, you play to win.'

Emilio got to his feet.

'So long as that's clear. I also prefer to play fair,' he said obscurely.

And before she could demand an explanation, the oxygen supply gave out altogether.

It was not polished and it was not seductive. But it was very efficient.

One moment she was standing there, hugging herself and flinching under his basilisk displeasure. The next she was in his arms. She had not even seen him move. But he prized her arms apart and clipped them ruthlessly behind her back.

And then he was kissing her.

Abby's thoughts whirled.

His mouth was hard. His body was hard. His chest felt like an iron grille. The constraining hand at her wrists gripped like a vice.

But...

But...

All the experience of the last nine years dissolved, as if she had never known any other man. As if in a dream, Abby stood there and let him feast on her mouth.

She thought, Why didn't I remember that it felt like this?

She thought, He feels like an alien. Why don't other men feel like an alien? It's exciting.

She thought, So this time he's kissing *me*. At last!

And then, in a sudden blaze of triumph, He's *shaking*.

She wrenched her hands free and flung them round his neck.

Suddenly his mouth wasn't hard anymore. Just slow and deliberate.

Abby ran her hands over his skin. She luxuriated in the strangeness of it, the warmth and the shocking sensitivity. His gasp of reaction thrilled her.

His hold tightened and she curved into his body as if she had been designed for it.

Yes, she said silently.

He raised his head.

'Abby.' His voice sounded strangled.

'Yes,' she said aloud. She ran her lips down the long, powerful length of his neck. 'Mmm?'

'Abby, stop for a moment.' The accent was husky.

Not talking like a machine gun anymore, thought Abby with satisfaction. She ran her tongue along his collar bone. Emilio groaned.

Abby smiled secretly. 'Stop? Why?' she said, absorbed.

'We need to talk,' he said on a rising inflection.

Abby was experimenting.

'No, we don't,' she murmured, not deflected. 'Talking is a seriously bad idea. When we talk we shout. Absolutely no more talking.'

In desperation he seized her and held her away from him.

'Why did you do that?' she demanded, reproachful but not yet hurt.

For a moment he looked almost wild. Then he seemed to gather himself together.

'Because you don't know what you're doing.'

Abby gave him a naughty grin. 'No?'

He did not smile back. In spite of the golden skin, he looked pale. She gave a little frustrated wriggle but he held her away implacably.

'I shouldn't have started this. I was angry. But it is no excuse.'

Abby winced. But she was too aroused to stop now. 'OK, you started it. But I'm all signed up now. We can't just *stop*.'

She wriggled again. But he was holding her too far away for her to touch his body as she wanted.

Emilio's throat moved.

'Yes, we can,' he said steadily. 'I'm stopping right now.'

She did not believe him. She met his eyes.

'Why?'

He closed his eyes briefly. 'Because you didn't sign up for this, and neither did I.'

'But—'

He interrupted her. 'Abby.'

There was a deep note in his voice that she had not heard before.

'Yes?'

'Maybe we will be lovers,' he said quietly. 'I don't know. But not because I lost my temper and you had to see how far you could drive me.'

She stopped as if she had been shot.

Then, all of a sudden, she was not resisting his hold. She was pulling away with all her strength.

Emilio dropped his hands. He drew a long, ragged breath.

Abby retreated, until she had her back against the fridge. She did not say anything.

Well, he had done it, thought Emilio, watching her carefully. He had behaved well, in spite of all the temptations not to. Looking at Abby's stricken expression now, he wished with all his heart that he had not.

Conscience was all very well. And so was long-range planning. But he had hurt her. It did not take a genius to see that. Hurt her for the second time. He knew that, even if she did not yet.

Suddenly he saw that he might never win her confidence back after this. He was shaken by a gust of furious regret. Why hadn't his overactive conscience thought of that while there was still time?

He said under his breath, 'Don't look like that.'

Abby shook her head. Her blood was in turmoil. She did not know what she thought. She did not know what she was going to do. All she knew was that she had never been so humiliated in her life. Or nearly never—

Without thinking, she flung at him, 'Does it turn you on, winding a girl up so you can turn her down?'

He looked thunderstruck.

'What?'

'I don't know about your other ladies.' She was shaking inside, very slightly, very hard. Convulsive fury, she assured herself. 'But this is my second time round the block with you, you—you—tennis court Romeo.' It would have been ridiculous, if she hadn't been hurting so much.

His eyes flickered.

That was when Abby realised three things simultaneously: he knew; he had known for a long time; and he hoped she had forgotten.

She said flatly, 'I hate you.'
She walked out without looking behind her.

There was no key to her bedroom door. Not that it mattered,
thought Abby, slamming it and leaning her back against it.
Emilio had made it very plain that he was not going to come
anywhere near her tonight. If she wanted to be alone, that
was just fine by him.

She drew several painful breaths. This hurt much too deep
for tears. She felt as if she had walked into a furnace. And
was not too sure what had walked out.

How could he have known all along that she was the girl
in the Montijo's garden? How come he even remembered
that clumsy teenager, among his Callies and his Floritas and
his Rosannas?

She winced, going off on a savagely irrelevant tack as she
recalled Rosanna Montijo. The gossip column made it sound
as if Emilio had had a fling with her, too. And as if she was
married. Was there nothing the man would not do?

Well, yes, there was, she thought. He would not take Abby
Templeton Burke to bed when she practically begged him to.

A wave of desolation swept over her, as real as a cold
wind on a dark night. Not stopping to take off her clothes,
she lay down on the bed, hugging her knees to her breast,
huddling the duvet round her.

All through the night, she tried and tried to get warm. But
warmth eluded her. Like sleep.

As soon as the first glimmer of light was in the sky she
got up. Even a hot shower did not really warm her up, though
it got the blood moving again. And she knew what she must
do.

She dressed. Pulled her outdoor coat around her shoulders.
Put her key down on the hall table. And closed the door very
softly but finally behind her.

She had been into the offices of C&C early before but never
this early. She looked at her watch. If asked, she would have

said the deserted office would have been spooky. But she was beyond jumping at shadows. The emptiness was peaceful.

The first thing she did was send an e-mail to her father. She knew he would pick it up on his laptop, wherever he was in the Caucasus by now.

Hi, Dad. Sorry to give you bad news but you need to know that Justine has given me notice to quit the garden flat. I've been living with a friend. It hasn't worked out. I expect the stuff in the paper will catch up with you eventually. Don't worry about it. It isn't what you think. But I need to move on and that may get in the papers, too. I won't be telling them Justine kicked me out. But I won't be telling lies about it, either. I'll let you know my new address when I move in.

Love, Smudge.

Well, got that sorted, she thought. Odd how something that had been the most important thing in her life a couple of weeks ago should suddenly seem so irrelevant.

She went down to the lobby and picked up the morning papers from the heavy-eyed porter. Might as well start looking for a flat before everyone else in London got at the property rental pages.

'They got a nicer photo of you today,' said the porter kindly.

'Thank you.' Abby was turning away but she did a double take at that. She looked down at the untouched bundle of papers in hand. Then she turned back to him. 'Today? You haven't seem me in the paper today, surely? That was yesterday.'

He held up his own copy of the tabloid and grinned.

Her heart plummeted.

When she got back to her desk she did not even look at

the property rental listings. She went straight for the tabloid gossip.

It was bad. Today she was in all three of the big circulation papers. Tracy's Town Gossip led the pack.

'Heartbreaker Abby Templeton Burke wasn't taking calls yesterday, as her new squeeze, Emilio Diz, flew back from Spain unexpectedly. He wasn't talking, either.'

There was a photograph of Emilio, striding through an airport lounge. He was frowning blackly. Of course, Abby knew that in all likelihood it was a library picture that the paper had brought in from somewhere. But that frown still made her want to avert her eyes.

She forced herself to read on.

'A former country girl, the Fab Ab has been really making her mark since she hit town in the autumn. And turning into a raver while she did it. Check out the education of an It girl.'

There followed a series of four photographs, labelled October through January. The picture editor had done a good job. He must have been working from the sheets of photographs of publicity events with literally thousands of pieces to choose from. His selection was skilfully designed to show Abby progressively breaking away from pearl earrings and timeless classics to C&C's idea of tomorrow's fashion.

And, of course, she was with a different man in each picture. No matter that at least one she had talked to only for the five minutes it took to take the photograph. No matter that one was a C&C client and another was her boss. The list made her look like a heartless butterfly. And that was being generous.

Racing driver... Industrialist... Art collector... That was her boss. Presumably they thought it spoiled the story if they said she worked for him and attending that particular function had been part of her job, thought Abby ironically. *Lead singer with the Spiro brothers...*

'Deor,' muttered Abby aloud.

It made it look as if she had taken a different lover every month. The photograph they had got of her made it worse, somehow. It was a studio portrait that her father had had taken for her twenty-first birthday. 'One for the top of the piano,' the family had teased.

It was all soft focus and made her look uncharacteristically dreamy. Her eyes were wide and her full mouth slightly parted. As far as Abby recalled, the photo session had gone on for ever and, by the time he took that one, she was beginning to drift away with boredom, which accounted for the dreamy look. But her father had loved it. And, next to the rogues' gallery of her supposed lovers, her expression was not so much dreamy as—well, frankly, sensuous.

Abby felt herself go hot.

She would have given up reading there and then if there had not been banner flash under the photograph.

'Tying yourself down. Girls, do you need to? See how you voted, page 8&9.'

Abby felt sick.

CHAPTER TEN

EMILIO was not surprised to find the key on the hall table. Angry, yes, mainly with himself. But not surprised. He could not have handled it worse.

All that debating about when he should tell her that they had met before! About how he had felt and how he had remembered! How could he ever have thought he had any control over it?

Once they started yelling at each other, any sensible game plan had gone out of the window. The die was cast. It was a sure-fire certainty that they would do just what they had done—fall into each other's arms as if they were starving. After that, the revelation was inevitable.

And she had remembered, too. He was not prepared for that. It was one of the many things that had thrown him, making him brutally high-handed when all he had wanted—

He broke out in a sweat remembering what he had wanted. What, for a few earth-shaking minutes, Abby had wanted, too.

Well, he had tried to be responsible. With the result that now she hated him. He wasn't too keen on himself, either.

I should have taken her to bed, he thought. I should never have tried to be noble.

C&C reaction to Abby's new notoriety varied from indifference to hilarity. Molly di Perretti, alone, seemed to realise that Abby might actually mind. And even she did not think there was anything to be done.

'It will blow over.'

'Will it?'

'Sure. There'll be another story along in a minute. There always is.'

'That's a great comfort,' said Abby dryly. 'Will it come with forgetfulness pills?'

'Oh, come on, Abby. It's not the end of the world. The columns are quite kind. They think you're great.' She looked at Tracy's poll and grinned. 'Heck even the punters think you're great.' She read aloud, '"Eighty-two per cent said, Ab is right. No woman should tie herself down."'

'Wonderful,' said Abby. 'Whenever did I say I didn't want to tie myself down?'

'Well, all right, they said it for you. But you're not looking for marriage, are you?'

Abby winced. She covered it up with a loud snort.

'Just as well I'm not.' She shook the news clipping viciously. 'After that little character assassination, I'm not going to get it, am I?'

Molly reflected suddenly that Abby might just possibly be serious about Emilio Diz. She was living with the man, after all, which she had never shown any sign of doing before.

'Well, maybe not with Emilio,' Molly conceded. 'He ain't going to like being told by a British newspaper that his latest girlfriend can take him or leave him.'

'Oh, you can see that, can you?"' said Abby, with heavy irony.

'Human nature. But there are other men.' She thought about it. 'Well, there will be when this has all blown over.'

'Thank you,' said Abby, 'That's a great comfort.'

She banged through her work with a crisp professionalism that quite cowed anyone she spoke to. Radio Scunthorpe did not even fight back. And a regional London newsroom found they had agreed to interview a fund-raiser for a charity they did not even recognise. On the point of ringing back, they received a full brief headed 'Questions you would have asked if you'd been thinking straight.'

'Phew,' said the researcher's e-mail of thanks. 'You're quite an operator, aren't you?'

But Abby didn't feel like an operator. She felt like something between a laughing-stock and a woman whose life was over.

But at least she did not have to be a turquoise-haired woman whose life was over. She went to her normal hairdresser and plumped into a seat.

'Turn me back into someone I recognise,' she said, looking in the mirror with shadowed eyes.

It was going to take more than than a new hair colour, she thought.

But she still had to have a roof over her head. If she had been reluctant to go to a hotel when Justine threw her out, it was completely out of the question with a bunch of gossip-hungry journalists looking for signs of the end of her mythical relationship with Emilio Diz.

She returned from the hairdresser; steamed through her work; and got on the phone. She had to have a flat by tonight.

In spite of what he had flung at her in the heat of the moment, Emilio did not really believe that the gossip writers would return for another bite at him and Abby. So he was astonished when the Madrid office e-mailed him the London press cuttings. And even more when Federico called him mid-morning with the news that he had heard it, too.

'So?' said Emilio uninvitingly.

'Is it serious?'

'Why?'

'Well, you seemed a bit distracted. Is this girl the reason?'

'Isn't that my business?'

There was a disconcerted pause. 'Yes, I suppose so.'

'Fine. Then leave me to sort it out.'

'Right,' said Federico, feeling as if he had stopped a cannon-ball without even knowing that battle had been joined.

The moment he put down the phone he called the siblings who were all waiting to hear Emilio's reply.

'It's serious. And it's not going well.'

'Good,' said Isabel in Argentina. 'It's about time. Women have always fallen at his feet. It will be good for Emilio to have to *try*.'

The family—who loved and relied on him—gave it their consideration and decided that they agreed with her.

Emilio, having to try really hard for the first time in a long history of romantic entanglements, did not know where to start.

He got rid of his day's work even more expeditiously than Abby. Then he freed up his diary for the rest of the week.

'Big negotiation?' asked his new PA, excited.

'The biggest,' agreed Emilio.

It was, he realised, true.

As always, when he had a major problem to resolve, he took himself off to the tennis courts. He had joined a club in west London just about the same time as he bought the apartment. Now he drove down there, frowning horribly at every traffic light along the way.

The professional was pleased to be asked for a game. He had had several trials for the national squad and was confident of his quality. Of course, Diz had been among the ten best in the world at one time. But that was a long time ago. And these days he was a businessman. Everyone knew businessmen were out of shape. No, the professional had no doubts that he could give Diz a decent game.

So he was absolutely unprepared. Emilio, simmering with rage that was only made worse by the fact that he knew he himself was more than half to blame for the whole mess, slammed the boy all round the court. He did not give away a single shot. He fought over every point as if he was playing in front of thousands, instead of two ground staff and a woman walking her dog.

The professional could only be glad when the uneven

match ended and he could get his breath back. By contrast, Emilio looked more ready to jump back into the fray again. His chest rose and fell evenly and he danced around lightly, shaking the tension out of his well-exercised calves.

Sheer ostentation, thought the professional sourly.

But he was won over when Diz put an arm round him as they came off court.

'Thanks. Let me buy you a beer. You have no idea how much I needed that.'

By the time he got back on the road, Emilio had his strategy worked out.

After her phone calls, Abby had a list of flats to view that night. All of her potential landlords sounded startled at the thought of her moving in at once. None of them sounded keen. But Abby, bearing in mind her victory of the day's adversaries, was not having any truck with that.

She negotiated with Sam for an early departure. Then left to buy a toothbrush before going to view her first flat. Abby set out briskly, prepared to do battle, if necessary.

But not with Emilio Diz. The moment she came out of the door and saw his car in the car park, all her brave determination fell away. She stopped dead.

He had seen her. He got out of the car and came towards her.

He was not wearing his business suit this time. He was wearing those sexy black jeans and a dark T-shirt. As she got closer, she saw that there was a sports bag in the back of his car.

She was astonished by her shock.

So he had been skiving off, she thought, grappling with the idea. Well, why not? He would not have cared much about what happened between them, or he would have come to her last night. Of course he did not care. She was the latest in a long long line of women whose names had been linked with him. And she was not even a proper girlfriend.

Even so, she was hurt that he had cared so little. While she had been unable to think about anything else, he had been out to the gym!

Abby told herself that it was typical male indifference. It was, she decided, par for the course. All right, it made her want to hit him. But it was not worth suffering over, not in comparison with their exchange in the kitchen last night. Now *that* was really unbearable.

Accordingly she turned abruptly and walked away from him.

He caught up with her easily.

Abby kept walking. 'Go away.'

Emilio kept pace with her just as easily.

'I can't. I've got to talk to you.'

'So you said last night. And I thought we did.'

'Yes but—'

'And you were happy enough that we had finished then.'

'What?'

'I was under your roof all night,' Abby reminded him, her heart too hot to be wise. 'You didn't have anything more to say then.'

Emilio's face twisted. 'Oh, God. I *knew* I should have taken you to bed.'

It was like a blow. For a moment she could not say a word.

Then she found her voice. 'Go away,' she choked.

He put a hand on her arm. Abby's heart lurched. She faltered and nearly tripped. He steadied her.

'Abby, I realise I hurt you last night,' he said simply. 'I'm sorry.'

'Thank you,' she said, her voice tight.

It was not convincing, even Abby could hear that.

She really, *really* did not want to have to think about what she had said and done last night. Especially not with him standing in front of her. Even though he had his clothes on now, she could remember a little too vividly the shocking warmth of his naked chest. And her own reaction to it.

She shook off his hand and said fiercely, 'Can I go now? Or do you want to have another go at destroying my ego?'

'I never meant to do that.'

Abby was writhing inwardly. 'Well, you hit the jackpot without trying then.'

She tried to push past him. He stepped in front of her.

He was still warm. In spite of the cold day and his light clothing, she could have warmed her hands on him if she had let herself touch him. She stuffed her hands in her pockets. Out of sight, her nails gouged crescents out of her palms.

'Abby, that's not fair.'

'Maybe not. But it's how I feel.'

His mouth tightened. 'I know how you feel. You made it very clear last night.'

I hate you! It hung between them, unspoken but as loud as if she had screamed it.

Almost sobbing—with fury, she told herself, with *fury*—she said, 'Then get out of my way.'

He said urgently, 'I told you I'd find a way to deal with it. I have.'

That gave her pause as nothing else would have done.

'You have? How?'

He was too experienced to relax. But he stopped barring her path.

'It will take some cooperation on your part.'

Abby hesitated. 'I'm listening.'

It was not encouraging, thought Emilio. But at least she was not actually throwing flames at him for the moment. He sighed. This was not how he had ever imagined making his first proposal.

But planning did not seem to work with Abby. He would have preferred candlelight and soft music. Hell, he would have settled for her not shivering with cold. But she was here, she was listening, and if last night had taught him nothing else, it had taught him to seize the moment. He might not get another chance.

He said abruptly, 'Marry me.'

Abby stared at him, blank. For a moment she thought she must have misheard.

'What?'

Ouch! Thought Emilio. But he repeated it, without comment.

Abby could not speak.

Emilio said reasonably, 'The whole newspaper story is a fabrication. We both know that. But the only thing that keeps them interested is the suggestion that you are two-timing me. We announce our engagement. They lose interest. It's as simple as that.'

Now, he judged, was not the time to add that he was wildly and unexpectedly in love with her; that he probably had been for nine years; that he would make it his life work to keep her safe and happy. He would save that up for when he took her to Spain. He would enjoy wooing her properly, thought Emilio.

He smiled at her in anticipation.

That smile was too much for Abby. She forgot how hurt she was in a blaze of grateful temper.

'How *dare* you!'

He blinked.

She was glad to see that something had rocked him off his appalling self-confidence, at last.

'You really do have to play to win, don't you?' she spat. 'Is there anything you would stop at?'

It was Emilio's turn to go blank. 'What?'

'Molly said you wouldn't put up with the press saying I could take you or leave you. She was right, wasn't she? That's what this is about.'

Emilio shook his head, utterly disconcerted. 'I've just asked you to marry me,' he said gropingly.

'No you didn't,' contradicted Abby. 'You *told* me to marry you. And I can tell you here and now, it's not going to work.'

'What isn't? What are you talking about?

'You don't play games,' she reminded him. 'Well, I don't take orders. I've had a lot of practice. Live with four brothers all your life and you become an expert in not taking orders.'

'Of course it wasn't an order,' said Emilio.

'Then learn to ask properly,' said Abby fiercely.

He shook his head. 'Oh, boy, this is not how I planned it,' he muttered.

'That I can believe.'

She glared at him, chest rising and falling as if she had just run up stairs.

But at least she was still there. She had not taken the opportunity to speed off down the road away from him, thought Emilio. Some faint voice somewhere told him that that was significant. Somehow he could retrieve this situation, if he just found the key.

'Do you want me to go down on one knee?' he asked after a moment.

Abby flushed. Her eyes were very bright. Too bright, he thought.

'Don't laugh at me,' she hissed.

But still she did not go.

He nearly took her hand. Then decided it would be wiser not to touch her for the moment. Not until he had managed to talk her out of some of that fury.

'I'm not laughing at you. I'm trying to convince you that I'm serious.'

Abby made a very rude noise.

He did touch her then. Wise or not, he could not bear to see her looking so wretched.

He pulled her into his arms. He did not kiss her, just held her against him.

There was a cold wind but there was that amazing warmth again. It was not *fair*. Abby could feel his heart thundering under her cheek. For a treacherous moment it felt like heaven.

He said into her hair, 'Come home with me, Abby. We can work it out.'

She nearly stayed there, cradled against him, acquiescent. She nearly let him take over. She nearly *believed*.

If only he had said he loved her, she would have been entirely convinced.

But he didn't.

Oh, he was kind, thought Abby. The fight seeped out of her, leaving her bereft and shivering. A part of her was even grateful for the arm round her. It felt protective. His voice was calm and friendly. He was like a rock. She had no doubt at all that when he said he could sort out the press stories, he was right. He would be able to sort out anything he wanted to.

Including a girl whose kisses he hadn't wanted nine years ago and didn't want now.

Abby's heart froze within her. She straightened slowly.

She said, 'I can't bear this.' Even to her own ears she sounded frantic.

Emilio looked stunned.

He let her go without a word.

Of course it was not as easy as that.

Emilio avoided her scrupulously. But the press did not. Abby kept a cool smile pinned in place and pushed past them whenever they tried to intercept her. She refused to answer a single question.

She could not find a flat as quickly as she wanted, either. After Abby spent a difficult couple of nights dodging the press in small hotels in Victoria, Molly di Perretti offered her sofa bed and asked absolutely no questions. It was not ideal but Abby was grateful. It even worked—until the celebrity gossip columnists tracked her down there, too.

Abby was at an industry fair where a client was showcasing the very latest in fibreglass racing boats. She had been there all day and was beginning to look longingly at the clock. The fair closed its doors to the public at ten but she was hoping to get away before that. And then her mobile phone rang.

'Hi.' It was Molly. 'Better be careful, Abby. Bandits at twelve o'clock.'

'What?'

'There's a couple of photographers camped outside the front gate. They must have had a tip off.'

Abby sucked her teeth. Not everyone at C&C was as sympathetic as Molly. In fact only today Sam had actually said that Abby was wilfully wasting media exposure which could be used to good effect. Used by C&C presumably. So it was quite possible that one of the more ambitious members of staff, deducing that Molly was putting up their in-house celebrity, had shopped her.

'OK. Thanks for letting me know.'

'What will you do?'

'Find somewhere else to spend the night, I suppose. I don't fancy being door-stepped.'

But she was running out of options and she knew it.

She ended the call and stood looking at the telephone. 'Here's where I came in,' she muttered. Only this time there was no knight in shining armour to save her.

Or was there?

Her pride revolted against turning to him. Her head said that it was a crazy thing to do, she would only be hurt again.

But her heart—well, her heart wanted to see him again, any which way it could manage.

'He may not even be in London,' Abby told herself, torn between hope and trepidation.

But it was Emilio who answered the phone.

'Diz.'

He sounded crisp and businesslike. Abby remembered the times when he had been far from crisp. In fact, she did not think he had ever been businesslike with her. He had either been furious, as he was in that first memorable meeting at C&C, or frankly seductive.

She shivered at the memory and could not speak.

'Hello?' he said again sharply. 'Who is this?'

'Ab—' Her voice sounded strange. She cleared her throat and started again. 'Abby. I'm sorry to disturb you. Can we talk?'

There was a sharp little pause.

She thought, Oh, God, he's probably going out to dinner with someone. He'll be getting ready. She may even be there in the flat with him....

She said hurriedly, 'Bad idea. You're busy. It's all right. Forget it.'

'Abby,' he said quietly.

'Doesn't matter. I'll think of something else.'

He raised his voice. 'Abby.'

'I can easily—' She heard at last and stopped jabbering. 'What?'

'Talking was a good idea.' The deep voice was amused. 'Where are you?'

'I'm at Olympia. But that doesn't matter. I can come over in a cab.'

'I will fetch you,' he said flatly.

'There's no need.'

'Yes, there is.' There was an undercurrent of amusement in his voice that made her melt. 'You could decide that I am too busy and take off.'

'I won't,' said Abby, concentrating on not melting.

'I still prefer to come to meet you. When will you be ready to leave?'

'Anytime.'

'I will see you in the foyer in fifteen minutes.'

Abby flung stuff together in the most rapid tidying up of her life. Then she grabbed her tote bag, said a distracted goodbye to the client, and raced to the entrance.

She only just got there first. Emilio was there inside the fifteen minutes he promised. He must have run every single red light on the way to do it in that time, thought Abby. She said so. It was a relief to have something neutral to talk about.

'Of course,' said Emilio.

He smiled down at her. The look in his eyes made her heart shake.

Not such a neutral subject after all, Abby saw, startled.

He took her bag from her proprietorially.

'And I'm parked illegally, too. Let's go before the law catches up with me.'

He took her back to the flat at top speed. They swept into the underground car park like a whirlwind. He brought the big car to a halt straddling two bays, and seemed not to care. It seemed out of character for someone normally so well coordinated, who always did everything with such impeccable precision.

But Abby did not comment. She was too busy keeping hold of her own reactions when he helped her out of the car. She felt horribly self-conscious as he walked her into the building, one arm locked round her like a vice. But there was no one there to take note.

Emilio felt the tension go out of her. He had no trouble interpreting it. His arm tightened.

'Have the press been giving you a bad time?'

'You've seen what they write.'

'Yes.'

It was the first thing he looked for every morning. Traynor's management had learned to be grateful for it. Emilio's distraction had allowed them space to effect some rapid reforms of their internal controls without his actually noticing. Sometimes, when they went to his room to discuss the next step in restructuring, they found him staring out of the window deep in thought. Not very comfortable thought. Traynor's management were Abby's greatest fans.

'Well, then,' said Abby, pulling a face.

But he was as philosophical as Molly.

'It's not so bad.'

He was opening the door to the flat. He stood aside to let her in. Just for a moment Abby paused, meeting his eyes.

'But it's not *true*.'

His smile was crooked. 'That depends on your perspective.'

'No, it doesn't. Truth is truth. They're saying that you—that I—we—'

He urged her in and closed the door behind them very deliberately. He looked down at her, his eyes intent.

'They're saying we're lovers.'

Abby flushed brilliantly. She looked away.

'You see, I can say it,' he said quite gently.

She swallowed.

'Nothing to say?'

She folded her lips together, shaking her head like the awkward schoolgirl she had once been. She could not meet his eyes now. Even so, she knew he was smiling.

'Is it something to do with being English?' he said, as if he was musing aloud. 'You talk about everything as long as it isn't important. And tell the truth about everything except what you feel.'

That did make her look at him.

Stung, Abby said, 'I've always told the truth.'

She did look at him then. And the look in his eyes was more than a smile. Much more.

'I remember,' he said softly.

He slid her coat off her shoulders.

Abby's lips parted. 'I thought we were going to talk,' she said, dazed.

But she helped him take the coat off. She even shrugged out of her jacket without him starting it.

'Later.' His voice was uneven.

That deep shivering had started again. She would have been ashamed of it if she had not been absolutely certain that he was shivering, too.

He was wearing a dark polo-necked sweater. Abby

wrenched it over his head. Her hands shook. He held them pressed against his ribs for a moment. She stilled, absorbing strength, warmth, the total abandonment of his body to her. Moved almost to tears, she bent forward and kissed the pulse in his throat.

He made a small sound, shocking in its rawness.

That was when they both lost control.

CHAPTER ELEVEN

LATER, she stirred in his arms.

Their clothes were strewn around the hall and they were lying with their heads cushioned on a tangle of his sweater and her smart trousers, now creased beyond recognition. He held her against him as if he would never let her go, even when she sighed and stretched.

'Emilio,' she protested, laughing.

His hold relaxed a little. But only so he could raise himself on one elbow and kiss a lifting breast.

'Mmm,' said Abby, between appreciation and embarrassment.

He smiled down straight into her eyes. 'You're shy.'

'No, I'm not, I—'

'You're *shy*.'

He looked delighted. Abby gave up trying to lie.

'There's no need to sound so gleeful about it,' she said mock cross.

'Sorry.' But he did not sound it.

He kissed the other breast. Abby felt her flesh stir. She gave a deep sensuous shiver.

Emilio's eyes darkened.

'Bed,' he said.

In spite of everything he had just done to her—everything she had done to him—Abby blushed.

This time it was her mouth he kissed. Lingeringly.

'Come along, my heart. You'll be more comfortable in bed.'

In spite of her shyness, she ran her hands down the long strength of his back, enjoying his ripple of response.

'I don't think I could be more comfortable,' she said dreamily.

'That's because you can't read my mind,' Emilio told her. 'I give you fair warning, you come to bed now. Or you take your chances on carpet burns. Your choice.'

Abby sighed and abandoned herself to his master plan.

At some point during a long and sleepless night, she said in wonder, 'I never knew I could be like this.'

'I did,' said Emilio with satisfaction.

They slept at last. At least, Abby did. She was not sure about Emilio.

The last thing she remembered as her eyes closed, was him holding her against the steady beat of his heart. He was looking down at her as if she was somehow magical. The feeling in his eyes made her feel shy and proud and humble all at the same time.

She tried to say so. But sleep overtook her.

And in the morning there was no time to tell him anything.

The first thing she knew was a searing light across her tightly closed lids. She turned, groaning, and flung up an arm over her eyes.

'Sorry,' said Emilio, from the window where he had opened the curtains. 'Small administrative difficulty.'

Under the protective shade of her arm, Abby opened one eye.

'Wha—?' she said blurrily.

'You might feel more comfortable getting up. My brother just rang,' He was quietly furious. 'He is on his way from the airport.'

All blurriness left Abby abruptly. She sat bolt upright, the duvet slipping catastrophically. Emilio stopped glaring for a moment. His eyes gleamed appreciatively.

'I'm sorry, my heart. I tried to tell him I'd meet him for coffee but his telephone kept breaking up.'

Abby looked at her wrist. But she was no longer wearing even her watch. Emilio had removed it between slow kisses last night. It was, as far as she could remember, the last thing to go. She clutched the duvet to her breast and told herself there was no need to blush. After all, she was getting used to him looking at her like that.

'What's the time?'

'Ten.'

'What?' For a moment she even forgot the way he was looking at her. 'That's terrible. I should have been at work an hour ago. They'll think—'

'I rang them.'

'Oh,' said Abby.

She revised her estimate of what her colleagues at C&C would think.

'In fact, I said that you wanted a week off.'

'A week?' said Abby, startled. 'Aren't you letting me out of bed for a *week?*'

'A great idea,' he said. 'But that isn't actually what I meant. I want you to come to Spain with me.'

It was not quite an order, but it was not quite a question, either, Abby thought. She smiled at him lovingly.

'Why Spain?'

'One, I want to get you away from the press here. They're not important but they're a nuisance and you don't like them. Two, I want to show you the Palacio Azul. It's my private place. Three—'

Abby lowered her lashes in deliberate provocation. Twelve hours ago she would not have dared. Twelve hours ago she would not have known how. She looked at him from under them, letting her eyes wander down his depressingly well-covered body.

'Three?'

She loved his little ragged gasp of arousal.

'Yes,' he said roughly.

He came over and kissed her hard.

'Stop it,' he said, when he lifted his head. They were both breathless and the duvet had fallen to the floor. 'Three has got to wait.'

Abby gave him a last sensuous kiss and allowed herself to be persuaded out of bed.

In fact, once up, she showered and dressed quickly. She was anxious to leave as soon as possible.

'Stay and meet Federico,' said Emilio, disappointed and rather surprised.

But Abby was suffering from a recurrence of last night's shyness. She did not think she could face someone who knew Emilio better than she did. Not until she was used to this new relationship.

So she said, 'I've got to get my passport, if we're going to Spain.'

It was even true.

He let her go reluctantly. But he pressed the key into her hand before he let her over the threshold.

'Don't ever give this back to me again. It's yours.'

He took her face between his hands and kissed her thoroughly.

She thought he said, 'Like me.'

But she was not sure. And Federico was coming. And she didn't like to ask, in case he hadn't said it after all.

She had left all her personal papers in the garden flat. So she went back now. If Justine had changed the locks, she would just ring the doorbell to the main house until Justine answered.

But her key fitted. Abby let herself into the silent flat.

It looked oddly abandoned, although she had tried to tidy up when she left. The answering machine light was winking, too. It had to be for her, if anyone was ringing here at all. But Abby was strangely reluctant to play the message. It felt like listening in to somebody else's life.

But she pressed the button eventually.

For the last time, she thought, surprised at how calm she felt.

'Smudge, I don't know if you'll get this. It's Dad.' There was a horrible crackle. 'We've got phone problems, darling, don't know how long this connection will last. Just to let you know, I don't care what the papers say. I don't believe you would ever do anything underhand. Whatever you do, you have my support. I'm back on the twentieth. Don't do anything drastic until then.' Another ear-splitting crackle. But even over half the world's static, the affection came through loud and clear as he ended in rough voice, 'Chin up, Smudge. We've got through worse.'

And then the line broke up altogether.

Abby stared at the sagging sofa. Her eyes pricked. Dear Dad. Dear, sensible supportive Dad.

But—don't do anything drastic?

Too late for that, Dad, she thought, smiling through the blur of tears.

She looked round the dusty room that had been home for months. It felt strange. Smaller than she remembered and somehow irrelevant.

It's not my home, anymore, thought Abby on a flash of realisation. It was. And I was happy. And it's in the past now. My home is wherever Emilio is.

And, out of her subconscious the truth that had been there ever since she saw him again, strode forward into the light at last.

I'm in love with him.

She sat down, with her passport clasped to her breast, and let the new idea take hold. It was like being in sunshine suddenly. Blissfully, utterly, inevitably *right*.

'I love him,' she said aloud.

She rushed back to him, bubbling over with the need to tell him. But he was not there.

Instead, a younger, neater, less rangy version of him was

sitting at the breakfast bar, reading his way moodily through a German newspaper.

'Oh,' said Abby, halting in the doorway.

The neater version stood up and smiled. When he smiled, he looked like Emilio might have as a boy. Not too fierce an advance guard from the family then, Abby thought, relaxing.

'You must be Abby.' He held out his hand. 'We've been waiting to meet you. Sorry to break in on you like this.'

Abby shook his hand, bewildered. 'But isn't that the reason you're here? To check up on me.'

He looked shocked.

'Good God, no. Emilio would kill me for interfering in his life.'

Abby thought of Emilio's expression when he opened the curtains this morning. She grinned. 'I suppose he would.' She looked round. 'Where is he?'

'The porters rang. They wanted him to move his car. Not well parked last night, apparently.'

Abby suppressed a reminiscent purr. 'No,' she agreed. She banished the memories. 'So why have you come over? Not a crisis, I hope.'

'Well, in a way. For me. I still haven't got up the courage to tell Emilio yet. I don't know what he'll say.'

Abby sat down at the breakfast bar.

'Then practise on me,' she invited.

It was very simple, as it turned out. Federico did not want to be an investment banker anymore. He wanted to teach.

Abby stared. 'So what is wrong with that?'

'Well, I cost Emilio a fortune. We all did. Not just in money.'

Suddenly, it seemed as if she had released a spring in Federico. Words poured out of him, like a dam bursting.

'He had to give up international tennis to look after us, you know. And he was good. Really good. My sister Isabel got pregnant but she was not the only one to have problems. I was cutting school, and Ricardo was very close to becoming a criminal. Emilio stayed home and got us all back into line. But it cost him his career. He could have been one of the greats.'

Abby did not know what to say. Federico looked at her with miserable eyes.

'How can I throw it all back in his face? How can I say, "Thank you for the education and the career advice, but now I want to go home and teach kids who don't have the luck to have the sort of elder brother I had"? He will think I don't appreciate what he gave up for us.'

Abby found that she did know what to say after all. 'Did he ever say you had to be a banker?'

'No,' admitted Federico.

'Did he ever tell you to earn lots of money?'

Federico shook his head. 'That was my idea,' he said ruefully. 'I wanted to show him I could do it.'

'So what do you think Emilio will say if you tell him you want to teach?'

'He'll be disappointed—'

'Not the Emilio I know,' said Abby quietly.

Federico stared.

She stood up. 'At least, that's what I think. Of course, you've known him longer than I have.'

'Yes.' He sounded dazed.

'Talk to him, anyway.'

She went to the door. Then paused.

'I should think,' said Abby, with a long hours of shockingly total frankness vivid in her mind, 'you could talk to Emilio about anything.'

She heard the front door open. Her heart swung wildly.

He's here.

And then—*I'm in love with him.*

Her lips parted, in silence astonishment.

This is the first time I'll have seen him knowing I'm in love with him. I can't do it in front of somebody else. I just can't.

'I'll leave you to it.'

She dived for her own old room.

She was aware of a burning shyness. It came out of no-where when she remembered that moment of revelation in the flat. She might be in love. But was Emilio?

What was more, though she did not know why, she sud-denly could not bear for Emilio to find her talking to his brother. Worse, talking about him.

It was as if she had asserted rights that he had not given her. After all, she was not a member of the family. He had not asked her to be. The only time he had talked to her about his family, she had accused him of being a cold-hearted play-boy. Abby pressed burning hands to her cheeks, remembering it.

Just because Emilio now knew every inch of her body, as she knew his, it did not mean that he wanted her in the rest of his life. Had he not told her that he could not afford a wife? That his shareholders would not tolerate it? None of that would have changed, no matter how much his chivalry prompted him to ask her to marry him.

And her being in love with him was an irrelevance.

No, face the truth, Abby. You've been talking to Federico as if you belong to his brother Emilio. More, as if his brother Emilio belongs to you. But get rid of the good manners and the explosive sex, and fundamentally you are just a girl who has spent one night with him.

She leaned her hot forehead against the window. She stared at the garden court below, not seeing the small early iris, the newly blooming daffodils. Not seeing anything.

Of course that was what she was. He did not care what the papers said about her because it was basically true. Oh, he had asked her to marry him, all right. But that was just a ploy to get rid of journalists. He did not even care about them. It was that lethal protectiveness again.

I don't want him to protect me, thought Abby, in painful discovery. I want him to *love* me.

But if he loved her he would have asked her to marry him

and meant it. Asked her last night, when she would have agreed in a second. When she was in his arms and surrendering every last secret to him. Surrendering gladly.

Surely he must have known that, a man of his experience? Of course he had known it.

So if he had not asked her to marry him last night, it was because he did not want to.

Face it, she told herself. Live with it. He calls you his heart but he never said he loved you. And he said almost everything else last night. So if he didn't say it, he didn't feel it.

Go to Spain with him, fine. Enjoy what you can while you can. One day you will join the list of Callies and Floritas and Rosannas in the columnists' files on Emilio Diz. If you can't face that, get out now.

But she did not.

There were tears she did not remember crying on her cheeks. She listened to the blur of male voices beyond the hall and did not move.

Emilio knocked on her door.

She called, 'Come in' but did not turn round.

'Got your passport?'

'Yes.'

He did not seem to notice anything wrong.

'I've got us on a flight at one. We're in first class and we'll only take hand baggage. So there will be minimal check-in. Still, we're cutting it fine. Can you do it?'

Abby steadied her voice. Could she do it? Of course she could. If you were in love, you took what you could get and gave all you were allowed to give for as long as you could manage.

'I can do it.'

Emilio hesitated. 'Are you all right?'

'Yes.'

'Great.' He sounded on top of the world 'Well, then. Five minutes to pack and then we're off on the big adventure.'

When he said five minutes, that's what he meant. Abby

stuffed washing things and a change of clothes into a bag at random.

This time he did not knock. He came into the room as if he had every right to walk in on her without hesitation. As perhaps he had now.

He looked vibrant with barely curbed energy.

'Ready?'

Abby swallowed. No, of course she was not ready. She was about to shatter her whole life. How could you be ready for that?

She brushed the tearstains away surreptitiously. Straightened. Turned.

'Let's go,' she said quietly.

CHAPTER TWELVE

ABBY had been half afraid that the press would trace them, either to the airport in London or in Granada. But she should have realised that Emilio would arrange everything more efficiently than that. At the Spanish airport they transferred from their first-class seats to a waiting helicopter without even entering the airport building.

Her passport was whisked away on the outward flight and returned to her on the helicopter.

'How clever of you not to bring too much luggage,' said Emilio, tucking a frond of hair behind her ear possessively.

Abby grinned. 'Like you gave me so long to pack.'

'And you rose to the challenge magnificently. What a team we make.'

Abby's grin faded. 'Sure.'

He looked at her shrewdly. 'What is it?'

'I—er—I've never been in a helicopter before,' said Abby. 'I think I'm probably a bit scared.

'No need.'

'I know.' She had pulled herself together. 'I'm not usually such a scaredy-cat. Sorry.'

'Don't apologise. It gives me a great excuse to hold your hand.'

And he did, all the way there.

The Palacio Azul was a surprise. It was not a palace, for one thing, but a two-storey farmhouse, built round a central courtyard. For another thing, it was not blue but white, with a scarlet-tiled roof. And for a third, it was on the top of a mountain peak, or so it seemed to Abby.

'This is the middle of nowhere,' she gasped, as the helicopter lowered itself onto a flat area of tarmac behind the house.

'It's private,' conceded Emilio. 'That's why I bought it.'

'I thought you were supposed to be turning it into a sports complex,' said Abby. 'That's what the Montijos said.'

And then blushed to her ears as she realised how revealing it was that she should remember such an insignificant detail from that encounter nine years ago.

Emilio raised his brows. But all he said was, 'That was the land on the coast. I've always kept the house just for me. It was the first place I ever owned where there were trees.'

He helped her out of the helicopter and ran with her into the house. The helicopter took off again. As the sound of the ailerons died away, Abby thought she had never heard such silence in all her life.

'Are we alone?'

'I thought you would prefer it,' said Emilio. 'I told the couple who look after the home farm to get in food and leave us on our own. But I can change that if you'd rather be waited on hand and foot.'

Abby swallowed. 'No'

But it was still rather alarming to be so completely isolated with him.

'Abby, what's wrong?' he said quietly. 'Have you changed your mind?'

She shook her head. What would he say if she said, 'No. Just fallen in love with you'? Abby wondered.

How long was she going to be able to keep that secret? She had not kept anything else from him. She had not wanted to. But this was one secret he would not want to know, she thought sadly.

This game of theirs was so fragile. Falling in love was too real. Falling in love would spoil the fantasy.

So when he said, 'Let me show you my trees,' she put her

hand in his and went with him like a careless nymph following a god into his bower, heedless of the consequences.

It was nearly dark. There was chill in the air under the trees. Abby shivered.

Emilio took off his jacket and swung it round her shoulders. It smelled of him, that elusive, utterly individual fragrance of skin and clean cotton and books that she would now always associate with him. In pure instinct, she rubbed her face in it, holding the collar up to her nose like a fine cigar.

His arm tightened.

'She's back,' he said in an odd voice.

Abby did not understand. 'What?'

'The girl who lectured me on the scent of roses.'

'*Oh.*'

She had forgotten that. She had remembered dancing with him. She had remembered the stars, the kiss, the rejection. But not those moments in the hidden garden while she told him about her home and he had listened almost hungrily.

Emilio said quietly, 'I could see them, those old roses. There were no roses where we lived. No trees. Your life could not have been more different from mine. And yet—it was extraordinary. Like finding the other half of myself. The person who had done the things I hadn't. And could somehow share them with me.'

Abby's heart beat hard. She turned to him in the gathering dusk.

'It was important to you,' she said on a note of wonder.

'You have no idea how important.'

'Tell me.'

He struggled to put it into words.

'You have to understand that I was not in a good mood. I was burning up with resentment. My family was falling apart and I had to do something about it. But—that meant giving up everything I had worked for. And I had worked, by God.'

'I know,' Abby said quietly. 'Federico said.'

He sent her a quick unsmiling look.

'Then maybe you can imagine how vicious I was feeling. I had to let people like the Montijos patronise me because I wanted to do business with them. From their point of view I was just one up from a performing monkey. They would ask me to dinner and then expect me to put on an exhibition match to pay for my supper.'

Abby stepped closer. 'Horrible,' she said vehemently.

Emilio laughed. 'Actually, it wasn't as bad as I'd started to think. Felipe was fine. We're still friends. Some of the younger women were a bit—predatory.'

Abby remembered the knowing conversation in Rosanna's bedroom. 'I remember.'

'I didn't like women of that class very much. And I'd got used to protecting myself from teenage groupies. And then I walked out into the garden that night and there you were.'

'I'm beginning to see,' she said slowly.

'You were everything I'd learned to mistrust,' Emilio said very seriously. 'And then, suddenly, everything I wanted.'

'*Oh!*' said Abby again, on a long note of wonder.

He took her hands.

'You were too young and I was too mixed up and it could never have worked. But I never forgot, my heart, my life. All the time I've played the field, just like that damned newspaper said, it was because I knew that second-best was never going to do and I didn't want any woman to break her heart over me. So I kept it strictly for fun.'

The Callies, the Floritas, even the Rosannas slid over the horizon. Abby felt as if a great weight had lifted from her heart.

At last she dared to say it. 'Do you love me?'

Emilio did not hesitate so much as a heartbeat. 'Forever.'

Abby trembled. But she believed him. She found she was trembling *because* she believed him. It seemed the most important thing that she had ever done.

'It seems so—unlikely.'

He misunderstood.

'I'll prove it to you,' he said urgently.

'What?'

'Come with me.'

He seized her hand and ran her back to the house. Once there, he took her through the shadowed rooms into the cool tiled sitting room. At one end there was a glass cabinet. He switched on a table lamp to show it to her.

Abby shook her head bewildered.

'Your tennis medals?'

'Only the first one. This is the important stuff.'

She bent forward.

There was a gold medallion on a stiff blue ribbon. The other medal seemed to be for life saving. On the next shelf there was a tennis racquet, its strings grey with use. A certificate which said Emilio Arturo Diz was a licensed pilot. A parchment deed of some sort, sealed with a huge red wax blob and silk strings. And a shoe.

A shoe?

Abby leaned forward, staring.

It was very high-heeled, cracked with nine years incarceration, strappy and delicate. She had hated those shoes so much. And he had found the one she kicked off and kept it all these years.

Abby found herself forgiving Rosanna Montijo, all seventeen-year-old girls and even ankle-breaking stiletto heels. She turned and found herself in his arms.

'Emilio Diz, you're a romantic,' she said, her voice full of tender laughter.

He was surprised. 'Of course.'

'And you love me.'

The arms round her waist tightened until she winced. But she did not complain. She leaned into him, breathing in his scent of him, knowing her power. And his.

She said quickly, bravely, 'Ask me to marry you again.'

'I am going to. I always wanted to do it here, among my trees.'

She moved in his arms. 'Then take me outside. Now. Quickly.'

Emilio caught her urgency. He almost ran her through the silent house.

The sky was purple-black. A soft wind curled off the neighbouring peaks and stirred her hair. The stars glittered. In the shadows, his body was just as she had remembered all these years, strong and fiercely controlled.

'Marry me,' he said in a shaken undervoice.

Abby put her arms round him. She did exactly what she had done all those years ago. Kissed him, without reserve. With total passion. With her whole heart.

And he did what he had done in her dreams ever since. He kissed her back.

Fierce, yes. Controlled, no.

Abby drew a long, long breath of completion.

'Yes,' she said.

CALL THE ONES YOU LOVE OVER THE HOLIDAYS!

Save $25 off future book purchases when you buy any four Harlequin® or Silhouette® books in October, November and December 2001,

PLUS

receive a phone card good for 15 minutes of long-distance calls to anyone you want in North America!

WHAT AN INCREDIBLE DEAL!

Just fill out this form and attach 4 proofs of purchase (cash register receipts) from October, November and December 2001 books, and Harlequin Books will send you a coupon booklet worth a total savings of $25 off future purchases of Harlequin® and Silhouette® books, AND a 15-minute phone card to call the ones you love, anywhere in North America.

Please send this form, along with your cash register receipts as proofs of purchase, to:
In the USA: Harlequin Books, P.O. Box 9057, Buffalo, NY 14269-9057
In Canada: Harlequin Books, P.O. Box 622, Fort Erie, Ontario L2A 5X3
Cash register receipts must be dated no later than December 31, 2001.
Limit of 1 coupon booklet and phone card per household.
Please allow 4-6 weeks for delivery.

**I accept your offer! Enclosed are 4 proofs of purchase.
Please send me my coupon booklet
and a 15-minute phone card:**

Name: _____

Address: _____ City: _____

State/Prov.: _____ Zip/Postal Code: _____

Account Number (if available): _____

---

097 KJB DAGL
PHQ4013

Marriages meant to last!

They've already said "I do," but what happens
when their promise to love, honor and cherish
is put to the test?

Emotions run high as husbands and wives
discover how precious—and fragile—
their wedding vows are....
Will true love keep them together—forever?

Look out in Harlequin Romance® for:

HUSBAND FOR A YEAR
Rebecca Winters (August, #3665)

THE MARRIAGE TEST
Barbara McMahon (September, #3669)

HIS TROPHY WIFE
Leigh Michaels (October, #3672)

THE WEDDING DEAL
Janelle Denison (November, #3678)

PART-TIME MARRIAGE
Jessica Steele (December, #3680)

Available wherever Harlequin books are sold.

Harlequin Romance®
Love affairs that last a lifetime.

HARLEQUIN® *Presents*~
Seduction and passion guaranteed.

Harlequin® *Historical*
Historical Romantic Adventure.

HARLEQUIN® *Temptation*.
Sassy, sexy, seductive!

HARLEQUIN® *Superromance*
Emotional, exciting, unexpected.

HARLEQUIN® *American Romance*®
Heart, home & happiness.

HARLEQUIN® *Duets*™
Romantic comedy.

HARLEQUIN® INTRIGUE®
Breathtaking romantic suspense.

HARLEQUIN® *Blaze*™
Red-Hot Reads.

HARLEQUIN®
Makes any time special®

THE AUSTRALIANS

MEN WHO TURN YOUR WHOLE WORLD UPSIDE DOWN!

Look out for novels about the Wonder from Down Under—where spirited women win the hearts of Australia's most eligible men.

Harlequin Romance®:

OUTBACK WITH THE BOSS
Barbara Hannay (September, #3670)

MASTER OF MARAMBA
Margaret Way (October, #3671)

OUTBACK FIRE
Margaret Way (December, #3678)

Harlequin Presents®:

A QUESTION OF MARRIAGE
Lindsay Armstrong (October, #2208)

FUGITIVE BRIDE
Miranda Lee (November, #2212)

Available wherever Harlequin books are sold.

HARLEQUIN®
Makes any time special®

Visit us at www.eHarlequin.com

HRAUSTR